This new award-winning colle ....
as a European master of the sl ....
metaphysical truths that lie h ....
wondrous in its situation and ...., ...
contains is hauntingly familiar in its resonance.

In the title story, four rabbis on a trip through the mountains offer marvellous and revealing interpretations of the similarities between snow and guilt, just before an avalanche, killing three of them, provides the most concrete interpretation of all for the survivor. In other stories, horrors await a scientist who provokes unrequited passion in a young girl; a wheelchair-bound philosopher rails at cosmic injustice throughout the events of the twentieth century; and a man who saves a kitten from death unwittingly changes his life through a random act of kindness. These stories, ostensibly reported by the author's former classmates, conclude with a tale of love written by Giorgio Pressburger's brother and fellow writer, the late Nicola Pressburger.

GIORGIO PRESSBURGER was born in 1937 in Budapest. He left Hungary in 1956 and settled in Italy, where he worked as a film and theatre director. He is now the Director of the Institute of Italian Culture in Hungary. He is the author of *The Law of White Spaces* and *Teeth and Spies*, which are also available from Granta Books.

SNOW AND GUILT

Giorgio Pressburger

Translated from the Italian by
Shaun Whiteside

Granta Books
London

Granta Publications, 2/3 Hanover Yard, London N1 8BE

First published as *La Neve e La Colpa* by
Giulio Einaudi editore s.p.a., Torino, in 1998
First published in Great Britain by Granta Books 2000

A CIP catalogue record for this book
is available from the British Library.

1 3 5 7 9 10 8 6 4 2

ISBN 1 86207 315 5

Typeset by M Rules

Printed and bound in Great Britain by Mackays of Chatham plc

CONTENTS

INTRODUCTION

I started my research seven years ago. I wanted to assemble all possible information about my schoolmates. A few months after our final exams, or more than forty years ago, some historical events scattered our class over all the continents of the earth. Anyone reading this little volume will find thanks addressed to my companions who remained in their homeland, and their names. The fate of five of us struck me as particularly worthy of note, and for that reason I decided to talk about them here. In two cases I have limited myself to quoting long letters which are published here with the permission of relations and heirs who wish to preserve their anonymity. Thanks to the son of a third, I transcribed a sound recording made some years ago. The two 'reconstructions' – in the form of stories – are based on scattered documents, newspaper cuttings, television broadcasts. I thought of giving this book the title of the story which is the strangest and perhaps the most mysterious: the suggestion came to me from the family of Dr Peretz, to whom I should like to extend especial thanks. All the stories contained in this volume are true.

G. N.

Affectionate thanks to my former classmates, for having shared with me the unhappy years at grammar school: Guglielmo Lukas, Gabriele Sarcozi, Giovanni Sarcozy, Giorgio Fabian, Andrea Hamory, Tommaso Guba, Giovanni Fandl, Pietro Gal, Francesco Sari, Sandro Giurcovich, Nicola Jordan, Ernesto Kormendi, Carlo Gimescovi, Nicola Davai, Desiderio Kalcio, Luigi Denes, Zoltan Petes, Ernest Schick, Tiberio Siclai, Ladislao Checikes, Giovanni Vagvolgi, Emmerico Farcas, Giorgio Wagner, Tiberio Deacco, Stefano Kozmai, Andrea Gulas, Giovanni Cano, Giovanni Kis, Pietro Turco, Bartolomeo Banio, Andrea Uhereczki, Pietro Hantz, Stefano Seculo, Francesco Timar, Gabriele Haller von Hallerstein, Gaspare Benco, Erwin Nosec and Stefano Metzger.

I would have liked to thank the schoolmates who appear in these stories, but with one exception, they are no longer alive.

SNOW AND GUILT

In memory of Chaim Peretz

Do not interpretations belong to God?

GENESIS 40: 8

The four doctors were standing at the foot of the western wall of the Gran Sasso. Guests of the oldest member of the group, Ismail Nepi of Rome, the Czech Hillel Goldstein, the Englishman Akiba Brooks and Chaim Peretz, an Argentine of Hungarian origin, had arrived from their respective countries on scheduled flights and by car. They dined together at the hotel and, after a quiet night, at dawn they prepared for the climb, well equipped and with adequate supplies. They were to decide which direction internal medicine should take in their own countries, and to establish whether such a branch of medical science could still legitimately be talked about. Shortly after their departure, as had been predicted, it began to snow.

'Like guilt,' said Hillel Goldstein, paraphrasing the book of Ezekiel.

'Fine, but in what way is snow like guilt?' asked Akiba Brooks.

They walked in silence for a while. All that could be heard was the crunch of feet on snow, and the laboured breathing of the South American Chaim Peretz, who was obese and suffered from catarrh.

At the first red and white sign indicating the path, after they had walked for about three quarters of an hour, Hillel Goldstein began to speak:

'Snow is like guilt because it covers everything, grass, shrubs, bushes: it covers everything with its white, glittering, apparently eternal mantle. Then, in the spring, everything melts with the first rays of the sun, the clods of soil drink up the snow that turns into water and disappears into the belly of the earth, into deep caves, into subterranean rivers. The snow disappears (as does the appearance of guilt), but the earth soaks it up, drawing from it nourishment to feed the beauty of nature, colours, flowers and leaves. Everything feeds on water as it does on guilt, which is absorbed, which becomes the essence of things. That is how guilt can be compared to snow.'

Hillel was thin and pale, frail flakes of snow had coagulated on his beard in clots of ice. He had spent a long time living in America, which he, in his bitter pessimism as a forty-year-old already touched by the pain of the first deaths in the family, called the new Babylon.

When Hillel had stopped talking, the group paused for reflection. Chaim Peretz, the Argentine, took a packet of biscuits from his pocket. No one wanted to eat them; they were all absorbed in their thoughts.

'Listen!' whispered Akiba Brooks. From a long way off there came a dull and uniform rumbling sound.

'Up there!' exclaimed Ismail Nepi, the Roman rabbi, tiny and rubicund. 'Up there! Look.' He pointed to a strip where the fir forest grew more sparse, and where a strange cloud of white dust was quickly advancing. 'An avalanche!' They all looked in that direction. 'It's been very cold over the past few days, but today it's about zero degrees, the weather is mild,' added Ismail Nepi.

'Yes, it's lovely today,' said Hillel. 'Fortunately there's no danger of avalanches here, the wood is too dense.'

They continued on their way with Akiba at their head, he having assumed the task of leading the way with his own footprints. The snow, almost three feet high, reached his belt.

They walked in silence for another half-hour. All of a sudden, fat Chaim Peretz began to speak: 'Snow is like guilt because it begins to fall very gently, in tiny fragile flakes, like little transgressions, little wants of attention first towards one's family and then towards one's neighbour; tiny guilts, practically infinite, like flakes of snow. We don't even notice them and then, as they settle on the ground with gentle fairness, lo and behold, they've covered everything. That's what the Book says: guilt is like snow. By the by, knowledge is like snow as well, and for the same reason: so many little fragments coming from

5

above, and then everything merges into a vast mantle. My belief is that without guilt knowledge doesn't exist. Animals don't feel guilt, and they know nothing.'

The group stopped for a moment. 'Skojah!' shouted Hillel. 'Skojah, you're a nice man, nicer than I am. Flakes of snow as tiny, filthy guilts all dressed in white! Animals without guilt and without awareness! That's lovely, really lovely!'

Everyone agreed with Chaim and they almost elected him as the best interpreter of the Scriptures. They continued on their way and after an hour's walk along interminable twists and turns, they suddenly realized that they hadn't encountered the red and white circle pointing out their route. They were lost.

'Strange,' said Ismail, 'we've taken the only possible path, there weren't any others.'

'It might seem that way to you,' said Akiba Brooks. 'It's the effect of the snow. It hides all roads with its "white mantle". Walking in the snow you can't know where you're putting your feet, when you're going to fall into a hole, where your steps are leading you. There aren't any right or wrong paths, it's all the same – uniform. You can only get lost. Peretz says that snow is like knowledge, but it's also like ignorance. You can't see a thing. You can do nothing but put your foot in a trap. That's why snow is like guilt. Because it obliterates paths,' concluded Akiba.

'The circle!' Ismail exclaimed at that moment. 'There it is!'

'Where?' asked the other three, almost in unison.

A few paces away, up the hill on the left of the road they were walking down, on the trunk of a fir tree there gleamed the red and white gloss paint.

'We've got to get back,' said Hillel. 'There must be a crossroads somewhere. Let's go back and take the path indicated by the circle.'

'What if this is the crossroads?' asked Chaim Peretz.

Finally, remembering the example suggested by Akiba, about snow-covered paths, the four doctors decided to go back to the sign by taking a short-cut across the fresh, smooth snow. But there was still the risk of bumping into invisible branches, falling into deep holes or into the hidden throat of a crevasse. After a brief moment's thought they decided to draw lots: the loser would walk ahead. Ismail was opposed to the idea.

'I'll go, I'm master of the house. If I reach the sign safe and sound, I'll give you my interpretation of the comparison between guilt and snow, seeing as I'm the only one who hasn't yet had his say. If I don't get there, on the other hand, it will mean that I was unworthy to interpret the Scripture. I'm off –' He set off slowly.

'Wait!' shouted Chaim. 'I'll go. You have to give us your version. The three of us have done it already. Come back.'

There was a moment of silence, then the little Roman rabbi, Ismail Nepi, turned circumspectly around and came back, putting his feet in the holes just dug by his steps. When he was back with the company, Dr Chaim Peretz prepared himself.

'I'm off, boys,' he said.

'*Mazel tov*,' said Hillel, and steam issued from his mouth like a little cloud.

Chaim sniggered with embarrassment, then set off. His robust form trembled with each step. The other three watched him, holding their breath. Now only Chaim's breath could be heard, loud and fast. His movements, on the contrary, were fearfully slow.

At a certain point, he plunged into the snow and vanished from view. 'Peretz!' shouted Hillel Goldstein, his voice broken. 'Peretz!'

'Where are you? Answer us!' yelled Hillel.

Akiba Brooks, like a good Englishman, kept his cool. 'Which of us is going to go and get him?' he murmured.

'Chaim! Answer us!' Ismail Nepi went on yelling, his keen and resonant voice beginning to crack with desperation.

'Dr Peretz! Answer if you can!' Goldstein modulated, imitating, who knows why, the sound of mountain calls.

'Here I am!' the calm voice of Chaim Peretz rang out unexpectedly. A moment later the doctor emerged from the snow covered with flakes. 'A hole. Nothing serious. I'll go on.' He went on walking, more circumspectly, more unsteadily than before.

'Here's another interpretation,' Akiba Brooks murmured, smiling and puffing. 'Guilt, like snow, makes us

8

wobble from right to left, from justice to injustice, with each step we take.'

'Hmm. Your interpretation's limping a bit, Brooks. Apart from the fact that Ismail has to give us his own before we have a second go,' Dr Hillel Goldstein observed with relief, looking paler in spite of the cold.

'Look! He's going to fall the next step he takes! I can feel it,' shouted Chaim.

'Don't be an ass, Peretz,' said Ismail. 'No joking about that, now.'

Five more steps and Chaim reached the sign. He turned around.

'I've been granted a pardon,' he panted. 'Come on. Watch out for the hole. Keep to the right.'

At that moment a dull rumble like thunder came from the summit. The three looked up, but in the sky which had, all of a sudden, turned grey, there was neither cloud nor sun, while the rumble had now become deafening, frightening. A whirl of white powder was approaching, small stones were beginning to rain down on the snow, the fir trees were starting to creak, to bend.

'Here it comes! The avalanche! It's swallowing everything, like guilt! That's what I was trying to say,' shouted Ismail Nepi. 'We're finished! Pray, sing, this is our final moment.'

The four doctors began to sing, clutching on to one another, but by now the rumble was extremely loud, earth, stones, tree trunks were rolling towards them, an immense, high and irresistible mass was approaching with a terrifying noise.

A moment later a rain of stones blackened the snow, the huge beast swept away their bodies, crushing and submerging them. The avalanche came to a halt on the plain below, like a treacherous wall that appeared in an instant, showing off its own dreadful dimensions. A second later, two helicopters suddenly appeared in the sky. Once the rope ladders had been thrown down, the first rescue team leaped to the ground, and its members realized that it would not be possible to find the imprudent walkers alive. Now, all that could be heard was the deafening sound of the helicopter. The three rescuers stood there disconsolately, in the wind thrown up by the helicopter blades and the mountain. They took out their spades and began digging feverishly. The other helicopter joined them and the second team immediately set to work.

After two hours they found the body of Hillel Goldstein. A boulder had crushed his brow, there was no longer anything human about his face. All that remained intact was the little body covered with snow.

After another three hours the men found the corpse of Akiba. It lay there curled up. Even in death it used its arm to protect its head, the bony box in which it guarded the most precious part of itself. A branch had pierced its lungs, running them through. All around, blood had dyed the trees and rocks red: and the snow.

At this point the men suspended their search: it was beginning to get dark and their torches were not sufficiently bright to light the place. They were heading towards the helicopters when a groan rose up in the darkness. Someone was still alive! Where was he? Who was he? They started shouting, calling all together. Still the only answer was the monotonous groan coming out of the darkness.

They lit the emergency lights. All of a sudden the Commander shouted: 'There he is! At the top of that trunk! Look!'

Then they saw Chaim, desperately clinging to a fir tree.

'Help! Please! Don't let me die here like a dog!' shouted Chaim in his South American accent. His family had left Spain four centuries before, moving first to Holland and then to Hungary, and finally to Argentina. Now the last of that long chain of the faithful was clinging to the top of a tree, which Chaim had just managed to clamber up in time. And someone had ordered that tree, marked with the red and white sign, to stand up straight and support the weight of the sensual, lively, foul-smelling rabbi, a doctor from Buenos Aires. 'I'm not dead! By some miracle I'm not dead!' Chaim wept in a loud voice. Immediately a helicopter stopped above him, a rope was thrown out like a noose; then Chaim's body, faint with terror, was hauled up and dangled in the air and the darkness to be carried to safety.

The cold was unyielding. The avalanche turned to ice, a wall tougher than diamond, a compact wall of guilts, seemingly eternal.

Hillel Goldstein's family arrived from Prague, and his wife recognized the little wedding ring that she had had made by a goldsmith from Mala Strana, by melting three gold teeth bought in a little antique shop. Inside it she had had her own name carved: Zilla, shadow. She slipped it from her husband's finger and wept softly, repeating, 'Muje malý! Muje malý!' Hillel really was small and thin, like a baby.

Akiba Brooks was recognized by his oldest son, Gerson, who found in his father's snow-soaked wallet a photograph of himself. He brought Akiba back to London and buried him in Kensington cemetery.

Ismail Nepi's family came: little Romans, curly-haired and dark, they seemed to arrive after forty years of blind wandering in the desert. They couldn't weep. Ismail Nepi's body lay somewhere, no one knew where, beneath the gigantic mass of the avalanche.

'What should we do?' asked Ester, Ismail's gaunt and spritely wife.

'Nothing, come back in April when the thaw comes,' answered the Commander.

Petrified, Ester and the three children's teeth chattered with cold. Then came the soft sobbing of a little voice, from Sara, the youngest daughter, Ismail's favourite. The child sobbed against that enormous pile of ice as if it were the Weeping Wall. A helicopter brought the family back to the valley.

Chaim was taken to a hospital in Aquila and slowly recovered. The injuries caused by the stones healed, the shock passed in the course of a week. When his wife and little children arrived from Buenos Aires he started weeping loudly, and all the patients in the ward complained; some of them laughed at his keen, loud braying.

Chaim didn't leave with his family, but wanted to wait for the snow to melt. He wanted to bury his good friend Ismail Nepi, whose body lay under that wall of snow, that wall of guilts. He met the insistence and weeping of his wife and children with a firm and serene refusal.

'What would Ismail say if he knew I was going to abandon him? He was supposed to be the first to walk close to that tree, and I stopped him, I made him turn back. I'm responsible for his death. I'm guilty,' he repeated.

He went back to Gran Sasso and took a room at the Hotel Imperatore. He spent his days in prayer, reading journals of gastroenterology and drinking a great deal at the Coachman's Inn.

There were two months of ice, alternating days of sun and storms. Chaim watched the avalanche changing shape, swelling, growing thinner. At the end of February it slowly began to melt. With his telescope Chaim looked for the first black stains of earth. One morning in the middle of March he woke up and looked out of the window. 'There it is!' he exclaimed. Big brown and greenish patches were emerging from beneath the snow. 'Guilt drags everything with it, but the earth and the sun don't stop, the great machine keeps working. We are all flakes of snow: one moment and all the good, all the evil we have within us disappears. Nothing has happened,' thought Chaim.

After another three days the dreadful avalanche, the diamond wall, the horrible wall melted. At dawn the doctor from Buenos Aires, once he had finished his prayers, woke the guide and confronted the mountain. Ismail's entire family had gathered outside the hotel: his wife and three children. Chaim Peretz approached them and began to repeat his litany: 'I killed him. He wanted to go over to that tree and I made him turn back. I killed him.' The wife and children weren't listening to him: they looked upwards. There were so many paths, up there. What was to be said to the guide, what places was he to be shown if he was to find Ismail's body?

There were too many roads and paths. Chaim called the emergency services and asked the pilots of the heli-copters that had brought him to safety to point out the place where the disaster had happened. The signs seemed too poor to the guide, who could not understand what spot on the mountain he was talking about, so he told Chaim to find someone else to accompany him. Then Chaim called the Commander and asked to be tied to a rope and transported to the spot where they had found him the day of the disaster. His friend's body could not be far away. He didn't want the wolves to tear him to pieces: he had to bring him back among the living and mourn him.

They spoke of the dangers and the expense of the expedition. 'It doesn't matter, I'm willing to do anything. I have to find Ismail: anyone would try to do it in my position.'

It was dawn on the first day of spring, it was cold. Chaim, wearing padded overalls, was hauled up on a steel cable and a harness under the belly of the aircraft. The sun was rising, the earth was damp with dew. Several times they flew over the point in the middle of the wood where the avalanche had buried the three doctors. Chaim was dangling in the air. Again he saw the snapped trunks, the obvious signs of the disaster, but of Ismail Nepi's body there was not a trace. 'The earth must have covered it,' thought Chaim. A strong wind suddenly arose. 'As it did that day,' it occurred to the South American doctor. 'And now, I'm flying like an angel, in the wind,' he thought. The two ideas connected in his thoughts. 'And what if he's been taken away . . . to the celestial palaces?'

He started to laugh. He laughed loudly. The pilot picked up his voice on his headphones. 'What's wrong with you? Are you ill?' he shouted into the microphone.

'No! I want to land!' Chaim shouted in his turn.

They returned to their starting-point, the cable was lengthened and the doctor was set down on the ground.

He sat on a rock and began to sob. The tears, sliding along his cheeks, down over his chin, disappeared on the collar of the overalls. He wept for a long time – all the bitterness, all the terror that he had in his heart melted into those tears.

'You too, Ismail, have been absorbed by the earth, like the snow, like water. And my guilt has descended to earth with you. I should have died in your place, and instead I've sent you to the slaughter, into the void. Into the void. Into the void.'

Chaim's shoulders shook as he wept. The Commander gave him a powerful tranquillizer. They took him back to his hotel. Then something unexpected happened.

That night Ismail appeared to him in a dream. He began to speak of the celestial palaces, of the angels. He named them, Chaim counted ninety-six names. He felt them rising in his brain, settling in its convolutions and melting away, disappearing. Ismail also spoke to him about internal medicine, giving him the solution to many desperate cases. When he woke up in the morning, Chaim had forgotten everything. His wife arrived at midday to take him back to Buenos Aires. Now Chaim was to return to his family, to live with his children, in his homeland, beautiful, wild and lazy Argentina. He was to resume the presidency of the Latin American Association of Internal Medicine, so that the little Roman rabbi could rest in peace wherever he was. Ismail's family said the same thing.

'He doesn't exist any more. Leave him in peace.'
Chaim listened to them and once he had settled up for his
long stay and the expensive exploration, he returned to
his patients in the densely populated districts of Buenos
Aires.

Weeks of happiness followed: Chaim's scruples left his
soul, and he enjoyed every moment of his rediscovered
peace as a father, husband, student of medicine and law.
Sometimes habit is like an anchor in the black port of desperation.

But after a few months, just as he was giving a trom-
bolitic injection to a shoe salesman of Polish origin,
Chaim remembered the discussions about guilt and snow
they had had the day of the disaster. Above all he recalled
Ismail Nepi and his disappearance. That night, filled with
a sense of great unease and fresh remorse, he lay awake.
He did not fall asleep until about three o'clock. Again
Ismail, radiant, happy, returned to talk to him about the
celestial palaces, the Veil of the Face, the angels made of
light and fire, the manservant admitted to the Presence of
the King, and also about new methods for curing hepati-
tis. But Chaim, as he told his wife the content of the
dream, couldn't remember a single detail.

Lia calmed him down: 'There's nothing wrong: dreams
are like that, they come and go. As for Ismail, it's your
duty to remember him, waking and sleeping, until he
finds peace. But when he has found it, on his long journey, then you'll have to leave him, your mourning and

your sense of guilt would only be a bother to him.' Chaim said she was right and inwardly accepted the nocturnal apparitions of the friend who had died in his place.

And thus, with a regular rhythm, every Friday night the doctor from Buenos Aires was visited in his sleep by Ismail Nepi, who revealed secrets to him and instilled science into him with a whirl of little flakes of knowledge. But Chaim, on waking, could never report with any precision what Ismail had told him in his sleep: he only remembered very vaguely, and by halfway through the morning everything had vanished from his memory – dissolved like snow.

Before turning to a psychiatrist or an expert of some other kind, the doctor thought of freeing himself from that nightmare in a natural way. At the moment of going to bed and kissing his wife goodnight, he repeated to himself that he had to rid himself, at all costs and for ever, of that nocturnal visitor, the phantom that his mind had created. He repeated it to himself every evening for three months.

'Leave me alone!' he finally yelled one night, in his sleep, in a rough and strident voice. 'Why do you reveal everything to me only to take it all away again when I wake up? Leave me alone! Go away for ever! Don't drag me into the abyss of dreams and knowledge, like an avalanche! Disappear! Disappear like snow, like guilt!'

Chaim's disconsolate cries woke the whole family. 'What is it, papa?' asked little Rachel, in her little floral nightdress. She had run into her parents' bedroom, and now she stood in the doorway rubbing her eyes.

Chaim, having returned to consciousness, called his daughter in his baritone voice, solid and safe once more. 'Come here, my angel. You're my dearest angel. There are no other angels.' He started kissing the little girl, whose childish grace made him forget his nocturnal visions.

For many nights Chaim slept deeply, dreamlessly: fully in accordance with the theory that the just man does not dream. 'You see, you see . . . It is not only guilt, but also that which is revealed to us, that is absorbed like snow. It disappears into the darkness of consciousness and the mind. And so we are tossed between revelation and ignorance, innocence and guilt. Perhaps there really is no consciousness without guilt. Perhaps knowledge and guilt are the same thing,' thought Chaim. 'Anyway, now I don't even know what the study of medicine consists of: it no longer exists. I'm not even a real doctor any more, I'm nothing. I don't want to live like this any more.'

He decided to take a holiday. He had to meditate, to rethink everything. He had an idea that he would make for the furthermost tip of Patagonia. His city's mild climate was annoying him. He wanted cold and snow again. One morning, after leaving instructions for the treatment of his patients, he said goodbye to his family, gave a big kiss to little Rachel, blessed his son Jitzhak, embraced his dear wife Lia and set off. He hired a little two-seater aeroplane, flew over the pampas and Patagonia, and five hours later he arrived in the frozen city of Deseado, in the remotest corner of Southern Argentina, not far from the South Pole. He put up at the Star Hotel, in a comfortable room that was kept improbably warm; from there he called his family. At five o'clock in the morning he got dressed and, fully equipped, he set off for the completely white desert plain. He walked for hours and hours without ever stopping.

The guide who met him on the final stretch heard him murmuring phrases in which snow and guilt obsessively recurred. He took him for a madman, for the usual eccentric tramp, and gave no importance to his soliloquy.

They found Chaim Peretz two days later, thirty miles from the refuge, lying supine on the snow, dead. His eyes were open, and he was smiling as though he had seen something beautiful. The police surgeon affirmed that going to sleep and dying in the snow can have that effect.

The doctor's wife claimed that Chaim had appeared to her the night of his death, telling her he had finally met Ismail Nepi and asked his forgiveness. In any case, without that guilt (of having involuntarily caused his death), how would he have learned from him everything he wanted to know: the names, the measurements, the medicine for all of man's ills?

But such matters, obviously, can have no place in an official report compiled by a police surgeon.

THE CASE OF
PROFESSOR FLEISCHMANN

His visage was so marred more than any man . . .

ISAIAH 52: 14

1

Fleischmann made his career in his own country. He didn't leave like the others. A study grant enabled him to spend ten years in America and then he came back. Over the last five years he has dedicated himself, in collaboration with a Trieste research centre, to the study of certain genes called 'homeotic', which govern the differentiation of the cells in the first stages of the development of an embryo. A year ago, one Sunday in summer, his parents and a sister died in a car accident.

At first Abramo Fleischmann's reaction was one of euphoria. He was constantly giving orders at home and at the Institute. He became more active than usual. One morning, through the glass door of the laboratory, he saw a girl dressed in a grey tracksuit, and wearing on her head a coloured scarf which held back long dark hair. She was leaning against the wall and staring at him. The secretary told him the girl wanted to speak to him urgently.

'Who is she?' he asked.

'I don't know,' the secretary answered, confused. 'She wouldn't tell me. A student, she said, but I don't believe it.'

The girl looked at him with big black eyes. Her expression was what is known as 'ardent'. Fleischmann was sure he didn't know her. His cast-iron memory didn't tell him anything about that face, that figure, that expression.

'Tell her to come back in a week,' Fleischmann said to his secretary.

'She wants to see you now.'

'Now . . . now . . . Everything can be postponed. Everything's a lottery. It happens, it doesn't happen, now, in a year, never. It's all down to chance.' Professor Fleischmann had closed the argument. He picked up the receiver to talk to an assistant: they were breaking down the chemical composition of one of the 'homeotic' genes.

He spent the day giving orders, organizing, delivering reports. He was in despair, his work all struck him as meaningless idiocy, or worse, filled with sinister and derisory meaning. Late that evening he left the laboratory on Walnut Street and got into his car. But he was too tired to go home, he felt the need to go for a drive first. He drove along the tree-lined streets of the Institute a few times, then set off along the sides of the Fishermen's

Bastion. All of a sudden he was gripped by the desire for a woman. Who could he call? Which of his girlfriends? His wife was in Hamburg at a neuropsychiatric conference on Alzheimer's Disease.

In the darkness of the alley the professor could make out a female figure. The woman's bare arms shone in the dark. A confident and provocative walk made her buttocks sway. What can her face be like? Fleischmann wondered. He accelerated a little and overtook the woman. He was unable to distinguish her features. But so troubled was he by his recent struggles that a sort of brainless and malevolent buffoon awoke within him. He pulled over to the footpath, lowered the window and called to the woman.

'Do you want to get in? I'll give you a lift. It's dark here. Come on, I'll take you with me.' He opened the door of the car. The woman, without a moment's hesitation, got in. Fleischmann, to retain some vestiges of gentlemanly behaviour, avoided looking at her and set off again along the dark avenue. He asked her where she would like him to take her. There would be time for everything: to see the forms of her face, find out her name, introduce himself, and the rest. Nice and calm.

A soft, well-spoken girl's voice answered: 'Take me to your place. Or come to mine.'

At that moment Fleischmann looked at her. It was the girl who had asked to see him that morning. After a few words, he seemed to understand that she was a former

23

student of his, whom he had completely forgotten for seven or eight years.

'I've read the text of your report. I think it's a discovery that will produce a new world. Its possibilities are unimaginable. A chemical substance governing the creation of the foot of a fruit-fly, transferred to the embryo of a rat, creates the feet of a rat. Transferred to man, it creates the legs of a man. And the same with the brain, with the heart. There's a bridge between all living beings. That substance you've isolated is the first of them. Others will come. The whole of creation is reacquiring a meaning.'

Professor Fleischmann smiled at her, leaned a hand on her arm and told her that that was precisely the core of the research: the universal meaning of living matter.

'You've understood everything, I'm glad,' the professor continued.

'You're very unhappy, and I had to do something for you, whatever the cost,' the girl suddenly whispered, quickly. 'I've got to save you. You're dashing headlong into catastrophe. Get off that path, I beg you.'

Fleischmann was appalled. What does this girl know about me? he thought. And yet that's the way things are, exactly how they are. I'm dashing into the void, into cynicism, into the pure suffering of nothingness. Neither pity nor compassion: just suffering. He said nothing of any of this to the girl. He smiled at her and asked her what it was in him that gave her the sense of an unhappy man.

'Everything, everything in you gives me that impression. You're living a false life, your spirit sees nothing good, only the spread of futility, of lying. It's all there within you. I beg you, save yourself. Let's see each other a few times. Let's talk. I can help you. Anyone can help an unhappy man like you. Come to my place this evening, please do. Come.'

Fleischmann looked at her. How beautiful she is, how intelligent and sensitive. In the meantime he could see in his mind's eye the harmonious sway of her buttocks, trying to form a picture of the girl's breasts, her pubes, the shape of her feet. Fleischmann felt a surge of his own virility.

'Where do you live?'

'On Danko Street,' answered the girl. 'Don't be afraid, come.'

'Where's that?'

'You know very well where it is. I saw you one evening watching those half-naked gipsies, those poor girls who sell themselves for sixpence. I live there. But I'm not a prostitute, even if it's terribly hard for me to find work.'

Fleischmann's curiosity was aroused. Where does this poor girl live, in what kind of house? he wondered. But ever-present in his mind was the girl's inviting body.

'Fine, I'll come with you. I'm thirsty.'

'Oh, I'll give you something to drink, you can have anything you like,' the girl said quietly, passionately.

They advanced into the dark belly of one of the poorest and most dilapidated districts of the city. Buildings that had once been imposing displayed their flaking walls, still pitted by the projectiles of a war that had finished in the middle of the century. For decades wooden scaffolding had propped up courtyards and decaying walkways. Fleischmann asked the girl only which road to take and she said 'turn right', 'turn left' or, at the last moment, 'no, please, go straight on!' They arrived in the desolate Danko Street. In front of a three-storey building, rickety and half in ruins, the girl told him to stop.

'I live here. It must have been a beautiful little building once upon a time. Look: two little towers on either side, the central body, the majolica on the walls . . . It's all been sullied now. But it must have been really beautiful. A little bit of invention in the fabric of a great city.'

'Yes, it's wonderful,' Fleischmann said ironically.

'The decay of the old isn't ugly,' said the girl. 'It's a prelude to reconstruction. And the same thing will happen to you. Now that your family is dead, it's your turn. You'll have to rebuild your life.'

'How do you know they're dead?' asked the professor.

'It isn't a secret. I read the funeral announcement. Don't be sad on their behalf. They were good people. Try to draw every possible good from what has happened. Come on. I'll make up for everything. I love you, I've loved you from the first moment I saw you.'

'Love?' The word frightened Fleischmann. 'Why are

you talking about love? No, I don't want to get into a mess.' The girl had already opened the ramshackle door and was waiting for the professor to follow her. Her headscarf, pushed back on her head as she got out of the car, gave her the air of a strange and exotic creature. With the light behind her the forms of her body looked even more attractive.

'Come on,' whispered the girl.

Fleischmann hesitated. He felt he was in the presence of a vague danger, but at that moment he was incapable of controlling his instincts.

'Yes. But wait a minute . . . I don't even know your name,' he stammered.

The girl came closer to him, took one of his hands and pressed it in hers. 'I want to give you everything you need right now. You're exhausted. I want to lead you out of that dreadful condition. My name's Regina. Come on.'

Fleischmann followed her along the dark entrance hall lit by a lamp hanging from the ceiling. On the walls, stains of mildew and filth had erased the white of the plaster. The stairs stank of cat's urine. Fortunately Regina lived on the first floor. When the old brown-varnished door opened, Fleischmann suddenly smelled the scent of sandalwood.

'Here we are, this is my house. Come in. I'm just going to the bathroom for a minute. You just look around in the meantime.'

Fleischmann stayed alone in the little room filled with knick-knacks, oriental fabrics, tinned meat, cups and little bottles. The furniture consisted of a folding bed covered with an antique fabric, a little table and two chairs, and an old black wardrobe, fluted on two sides. A little lamp hung from the ceiling. Regina reappeared, touched some machine in a corner, and the sound of medieval music pervaded the atmosphere.

'I'm studying singing. Eventually I'd like to sing music like this. I'm taking lessons from an old master, the best one around. It's very expensive. It bleeds me dry every time.'

The girl sat down on the little bed. She had put on some perfume in the bathroom. She gave off a very sweet, fine scent: heaven knows how much it had cost. But where does this creature get her money? Fleischmann wondered. He decided to get rid of any misunderstandings straight away.

'Have you been hunting me down all day to ask me for money?'

'No, I'm not asking you for anything,' said the girl with tears in her eyes. 'Absolutely nothing. Just for you to accept my love. I don't want yours in return. I want to give you my love because you need it. You're very ill. Let your spirit rest, calm down. Try to think that life isn't an illusion and a lie as you believe, but something infinitely better, something with a secret meaning, and you're on earth to discover that secret. Your intelligence is ready to do it, your spirit isn't, your spirit is groping about in the darkness.'

What's up with this girl, why is she saying all these things to me? How on earth does she know me so well? Fleischmann wondered. But there was no time to think. With a gentle push the girl made him sit down on a chair, slipped to the floor and began to unlace his shoes.

'Come, no one's ever been in this bed. You'll be the first. No, I'm not a virgin, don't worry, you won't have to deal with that problem. There have been people who have loved me to distraction, the last one a scoundrel, who did nothing but hit me to make me frightened, and I left him. All the worse for him. Now I'm alone, but I don't want to stay that way, I have to give someone all the good there is in me.'

'Let me be,' said the professor, impatient and frightened. 'I can get undressed on my own, you know.'

'No, you can't get undressed on your own. You would do it clumsily, untidily, or else too carefully. Let me do it. Calm down, let go, don't be afraid. Getting undressed, staying naked, shedding everything finally to give yourself is very difficult.'

Fleischmann leaned against the back of the chair and tried to calm down. In the end, what could possibly happen to him? This innocent and hyper-sensitive girl would be easy to disarm. If Regina – what a name! – made any kind of claim, he would deny everything. But now, why not grasp the sweetness of the moment, the grace of that body, stirred from the squalor of its surroundings?

Fleischmann rose to his feet and let Regina take off all his clothes, gently, caressing the parts of his body that were gradually bared.

'You're handsome. Why are you ashamed of yourself? Why do you despise yourself? You've even had the gift of beauty. Why won't you accept yourself?' the girl asked gently, pressing her lips to his chest.

'How do you know I don't accept myself?'

'I can feel it, deep within me. I perceive these things. I'll take the covers off the bed for you, lie down.'

She pulled back the fabric cover and the sheets of the little bed, far from immaculate, were revealed.

Do I have to mix with this base part of humanity? Fleischmann thought. 'I'm here now. I can't pull myself back. I hope it's over quickly. I'm never going to fall into the instinct trap ever again.

He got into the bed of the girl, who lay down beside him and suddenly swallowed and invaded him with her arms, her legs, her mouth. He penetrated her inviting body with some reservation. He felt her body's cavity open to welcome him. He tried to hurry up.

'Calm down, I don't want to take anything from you, I just want to give to you. Let yourself go, don't run away,' whispered the girl, responding to every movement, to each of the man's tiny gestures with a tender acceptance of his imagination.

The professor went home with a sense of euphoria mingled with indifference. He had already decided never to see her again, and in his heart he was delighted to have spent an evening that was anything but unpleasant. His anxiety had subsided a little, along with the black despair that had taken control of his mind during that time.

Two months passed and Fleischmann thought not for a single moment of that evening, of the girl who had offered herself to him so generously.

One autumn afternoon his secretary told him that a woman by the name of Regina had been trying to contact him on the telephone that morning. She seemed agitated. She urgently wanted to talk to him. Could he call her back? She had left a phone number. Fleischmann resolutely said no.

'She's a nuisance. She probably wants work. She'll be one of those people who always need help, they can't make it on their own in life. Tell her I'm in America, at a conference.'

Professor Fleischmann felt a certain pity for those creatures he had just mentioned, but as to doing something for them . . . They're an endless horde, he thought. Who could do anything to improve the fate of all those unfortunate creatures?

The call came again the following day, and the day after that. For six days, every morning Regina tried in vain to speak to her lover of a single evening. One

Monday in November, going into the office and receiving the same suspicious communication from his secretary, the professor decided to confront Regina and sort everything out once and for all. He arranged a meeting in the middle of the week. Fleischmann wasn't worried: just let the girl come to his office. He would receive her there, in the presence of everyone.

At the agreed hour Regina arrived: Fleischmann saw her through the dividing glass and barely recognized her. Instead of her tracksuit she was wearing a dark cotton dress, and a black overcoat. Dark glasses concealed her eyes. Only her long dark hair, held back in a multicoloured headscarf, was the same. Fleischmann's secretary accompanied her into the professor's office, casting glances of disapproval.

'Hello. Sorry if I'm disturbing you,' murmured Regina. She looked at the secretary, who moved away indignantly. 'I'm not asking you why you didn't look me up, why you didn't agree to see me. I'm only asking you to tell me if you've thought about what I said to you last time. You need someone to talk to you calmly, to take care of your health, of your happiness. Your wife can't do it. I've seen her. She can't understand you.'

'Where have you seen her?' Fleischmann asked anxiously.

'I've seen her coming out of the house, a number of times. Since that night I've come and stood below your apartment every morning. You've never noticed. I didn't want you to see me.'

'Are you checking up on me? Are you trying to harm me? Do you want to hurt me and my wife, destroy our union?' the professor asked with a hiss.

'No. Nothing of the sort. I want to help you, in secret, in silence, without anyone being aware of it.'

'Did you come to tell me that? And like this, dressed in mourning?'

'Mourning? I put on these clothes because I was on my way to a research laboratory. I'm looking for work, I wanted to be elegant. They all throw me out, send me away. No one wants anything to do with me. I understand too many things, they're frightened. And I don't want to frighten anyone. I just want to learn to sing. I need money for that. Music is the supreme good of the human spirit. I want to sing, lessons are very expensive. Help me to find work. Maybe here . . .'

Fleischmann felt reassured. 'A poor wretch asking for help. And I was frightened,' he thought. Then he haughtily turned back to the girl. 'Yes, I'll be able to help you. I'll try to. Give me a bit of time.'

'I can't. I've got to have everything sorted out by tomorrow. Today I only want to tell you that we could see each other, talk in peace, here, in a café, at your place. I want you to get better. I still see you as prey to negative forces. You know that negative forces exist? You mustn't give in to them. You're in danger. Please, listen to me, I beg you.'

'Fine. We'll see each other, we'll talk about it. But

now let's think about you. What sort of work do you want to do?'

All of a sudden Regina took off her glasses. Fleischmann saw her big black eyes staring at him in a kind of agitation.

'Do you hear them? They're saying bad things about me! Do you hear them?'

Of course. The girl's mad. It's better that I get rid of her, thought Fleischmann. And yet she's also telling the truth. How can that be?

'They're saying bad things about me. They're saying that you should kick me out,' whispered Regina.

'There's no one here. There's just you and me.' The professor tried to keep calm, but noticed a certain alarm in himself. The girl's obvious madness almost struck him as a performance, an attempt to move him to pity at all costs.

'I'm not mad,' said Regina. 'I know you think I'm mad. That I have hallucinations. Or that I want to make you think I do. I beg you, change your mind. Until you're yourself again. Those forces want to take you over. You think only of yourself, of your destiny. Leave this place, leave your passivity. Think about other living creatures.'

'Do you want me to think only of you?' Fleischmann asked ironically.

'I see you need time to understand that you're in danger. You're acting the lofty, superior man with me. Why? Haven't I been gentle enough with you? Have you forgotten how we made love? I'm going now. We'll see each other tomorrow at the Café Emke. At five o'clock. We'll have tea together and discuss your situation. You'll be able to confide in me all the things that are oppressing you, free yourself from your despair. Please, come. And tell me if you can help me. Devote yourself to it. I need help too. I can't wait. Help me.'

Regina covered her eyes once more with her big dark glasses, said goodbye and disappeared.

The next day the professor didn't keep the appointment, and made sure that Regina wasn't able to talk to him or communicate with him in any way. Two weeks passed and winter came. One evening, getting home late, Fleischmann sat down at his desk to examine the report on his assistant's last experiment. Among the papers he found a sealed envelope, the address handwritten in big, round, perfectly jewelled, rather childish letters. He opened it. Written in the same hand were a few words, repeated over about twenty lines in regular intervals: 'I love you. I love you. I love you . . . I'm your salvation. I'm your salvation. I love you. You love me too. You love me. You love me . . . Ours is a great love. Great. Great. Great love. Seek me. You must seek me. You must find me. I love you. There is no word for my love. For our love. Look for me.'

Fleischmann smiled. 'Poor thing. She's mad. I hope she gets better.' He tore up the letter, then, after a moment's thought, he got up, went to the bathroom and threw it into the toilet. He pulled the chain, and waited for the little pieces of paper to slip down into the pipe, to end up in the sewer, amid dung and filth, and then into the river.

My wife's arriving tomorrow, he thought. All I need is for her to find a love letter.

He went back into his study to read the report, and went to sleep with his head on his arms, leaning on the top of his desk.

He dreamed he was making love with Regina, quietly, effortlessly. He woke up at dawn with that dream in his head. Ridiculous! he thought, got undressed and went to bed.

The next evening, he found two letters from Regina on his desk. He opened them and discovered that he enjoyed reading these impassioned confessions of love. This time they were even more impressive, they spoke of their union, of their bodies, and Abramo was certain that, while she was writing, the girl was masturbating. He had never encountered such an overwhelming love in any of his women. Lia, his wife, arrived at midnight. They hadn't seen each other for a week. She was coming back from a conference in Jerusalem. They went to bed, embraced. Lia's love, compared to the one spoken of in the letters, seemed almost non-existent.

Maybe that's the right way round, Fleischmann thought. A true union is based not on the passions, but on clear-minded reason.

The next day he found two more letters from Regina.

They were inviting, subtle, they spoke of the love there was between them, as ardent as pity. Regina asked for help. To help her he had to seek her, to find her on his own. That was the meaning of their love. Each seeking the other. As two bodies seek one another with hands, with tongues. The help he gave to Regina would do him more good than it did her. Giving, that was the meaning of life. 'You have to come inside me. Into my body. With ardour and lightness, with wild passion and tenderness. Come, I'm waiting for you. My legs, my womb want to open up to you. I'm waiting for you. Don't waste any time. Life is short.'

Fleischmann was sorry not to feel anything like Regina's emotions and sensations, it would have been very satisfying, but unfortunately the time of such passions had passed for him, and anyway he would never have been so foolish as to ruin such a successful marriage for a momentary infatuation. Nonetheless, he didn't destroy the two notes. He would be able to read them, get excited, masturbate. He put them in the elegant leather briefcase that he took to work each morning.

But once he had reached the office, he changed his mind: he took the letters, tore them into little pieces, and threw them into the toilet bowl. Once again Regina's words ended up among the dung, the sewage, the filth of a whole city.

For a month, each evening, Professor Fleischmann received Regina's letters, now impassioned, now sensual, or rather lubricious, now filled with truth about life and the pain that had touched him.

No, the wound of the loss of our dear ones doesn't heal easily. In fact it never heals. Never, the professor thought one afternoon. He began to cry, looking at himself in the mirror of the bathroom where he had sought refuge. Everything dissolves, everything goes away. Who could replace my mother, my little sister, my father? How many faces, words, gestures, meals will be able to erase their memory? Why did they end their lives in that horrible and unexpected way, why, why? he howled in a whisper, looking at his own face distorted with pain. At that moment he thought of Regina.

She says she can save me. Maybe it's true. You have to listen to everyone in life. Perhaps she's right. I'll try to find a job for her, then I'll look for her. That was the plan dreamed up by Abramo Fleischmann to drive away his own despair.

Finding the girl a job as an analyst in a pharmaceutical company was not too difficult; anyone would have been happy to do a favour for Professor Fleischmann, a candidate for the greatest and most prestigious awards, thanks to his discovery of 'homeotic genes'.

He set off in search of Regina.

One evening, leaving the laboratory, rather than going home – Lia had dinner ready for him – he drove his car towards the dark, dilapidated district which he remembered accompanying Regina to months before. He also remembered the squalid and dirty street where, sometimes in the past, he had seen young, half-naked prostitutes standing. But in the maze of alleyways, badly lit and stinking, filled with drunks vomiting and shouting, he couldn't find his bearings. He returned home with a certain sense of relief, he had done his duty. His wife, who was waiting for him, handed him the nth letter from Regina.

'A nuisance,' said Fleischmann. 'Every day for two months she's been writing me passionate, almost pornographic letters. I've looked at the stamps; she sends them from a different district of the city every time. Who knows where she lives. If I knew I'd have told the police already . . .'

'Tell the police? Cases like this one often take time. In the end it might be better to meet her, to have her come here. I'd like to talk to her too. Do you know who she is?' his wife asked with a smile.

'Yes, I know. Why lie? One evening I even gave her a lift. She's a former student of mine. But I don't know her surname, just her first name, she's called Regina.'

'Look her up in the list of your students. You're sure to find her there.'

The professor decided to take his wife's advice. He took the letter and went to the bathroom to open it.

'Darling, you've reached the pit of your despair. Only my presence can save you. I know you're contemplating suicide. Chase away those horrible thoughts of death and

39

lies. Sincerity is love: it's simple, it's everything in this world. But all you can see is falseness and cruelty. You're contributing to it yourself as well. Seek me, my love. Last night I dreamed I was making love with you. I always dream of uniting my body with yours. It was beautiful. You were, as ever, tender and strong. All that is good in you must conquer scepticism and despair. Seek me again. I'm sure you'll find me. Sara.'

'Sara? Has she changed her name? What sort of joke is this?' Abramo Fleischmann came out of the bathroom and showed his wife the letter.

'This isn't just any old letter,' she said. 'The writing's a bit manic, but the woman must love you. And she's a poor, despairing thing herself. You've got to find her. Maybe you can help her. Who says you have to make love with her? But yes, calm her, heal her. Seek her. And that's enough now, let's think about us –' Lia tore the letter into little pieces, threw it into the rubbish bin among the rancid vegetables, bones and the rotting guts of a chicken.

That night husband and wife made love more passionately than usual. But compared with what Fleischmann had been reading in the letters for two months, their union didn't go beyond the normal routine of a petty-bourgeois couple.

The research that he had entrusted to his secretary didn't yield a result. Over the past two weeks no student by the name of Regina had attended his lectures, and there were only three Saras. When the professor called them in, none of the three turned out to be the girl he was looking for.

But something worse happened. One day Fleischmann didn't find the usual letter from Regina in the middle of his correspondence. The following day, and the day after, the same thing happened. Abramo summoned up within himself that dark interlocutor whom he had never mentioned to anyone, and about whom he had made so many conjectures. He had been sent a request for help, a fierce and fearful demand. He yearned for those letters that he hadn't had the courage to keep.

He felt lost. Not despairing or depressed; lost. Without a goal, without enthusiasm. His discovery was completed, he had worked day and night, it might well shape the future of humanity.

But what about the present?

Lia asked in vain what was troubling him. He didn't know what to reply. Could he speak of the void, of nothingness? Could he speak of his terrible longing for that girl he had embraced one evening, and who had disappeared forever from his life, leaving him dismayed? Could he speak of all those ardent words he had thrown into the toilet bowl? He didn't know what to do.

He took a day off. He went out into the streets which were swathed in a discouraging winter fog. He went all the way to the Octagon, he headed towards the Opera House. Yes, he had to set to work, he had to try to find a solution to his life. At the window of a stationer's shop he stopped to look at the photographs of a matriculating class: girls in white shirts, all their faces, sulky, cheerful, baffled, tousled. All of a sudden the reflection of Regina's face appeared in the glass. He turned around suddenly, his heart in his mouth. There was the girl, headscarf in her hair, tracksuit, little overcoat. His wish had been answered.

He didn't know whether to embrace her, offer his hand or kiss her. He stood there without saying a word.

'You see? You've found me,' said Regina.

'But I . . .' he stammered, confused.

'You looked for me and so you've found me. Are you coming to my place?'

Inexplicably Fleischmann was frightened. 'No, I can't right now. My wife is expecting me home for dinner . . .'

'I know. I don't want to put myself between you and her. But now you need my presence. And I need you. I've asked you for help and you haven't given it to me.'

'But I have!' Fleischmann said quickly. 'I've found you a job in a research laboratory.'

'A laboratory? I'm taking singing lessons now. And anyway I'm not a researcher. I don't know anything about any of that.'

'What, didn't you study with me?'

'No. I told you I did so that you'd agree to see me. I had seen you, I had followed you in the street. You were crying. I understood immediately that I had to help you.'

All at once everything became clear to him. This person really was insane. And he had given himself to someone like that, he had allowed himself to be seduced by a wretch who belonged to the dark depths of humanity.

'Let's go and talk at my place. Or in a café. Tell me how you are, what's still upsetting you. I can see the despair growing ever greater in your eyes.'

'No. I'm not in despair. I'm angry with myself for not understanding anything. And with that I bid you goodbye, I have to go.'

'Don't you want my love? Don't you want me to do all the things I wrote to you about? You'll never find love like this again.'

'I know,' Abramo Fleischmann said, lightly and wickedly. What did he care for that wretched love, those words? He had done the right thing in throwing them away. Words were no use now. What would they be for? New, useless illusions? Away with you!

He left Regina in the street, still murmuring, 'I'll try to do something for you. I don't want you to ruin yourself. You find every excuse you can to do it. Go beyond appearances, I beg you. For your own good.'

Abramo Fleischmann didn't want to listen to another word and hurried away.

2

That encounter, apparently casual and in reality so strongly desired, his own reticence, Regina's obstinacy, shook Professor Fleischmann deeply. But only for a few days. By dedicating himself to his work, throwing himself into his research, he gradually forgot everything.

At five o'clock one morning the telephone rang. 'There, they'll have found the second protein I was looking for!' thought Abramo Fleischmann. He had arranged with his assistant that at the end of the night's work he would let him know the result of the analysis. He picked up the phone with his heart in his mouth. He was about to pluck the fruits of five years of research. After a second a female voice whispered: 'Now you have to come and look for me. Number 6 Danko Street. I have something very important to tell you.'

'Who is it? Who are you looking for?' Fleischmann asked irritably.

'You looked for me and now I'm looking for you. It's Regina.'

Fleischmann hung up. 'That's it!' he thought. 'The thoughtlessness of a moment is causing you all this harm! This strange girl emerges from the night of time. How can you free yourself of a bloodsucker like that?'

A moment later the telephone rang again.

'Who is it?' asked Lia, stirring from her sleep.

'No one. Wrong number,' answered Abramo. Then he picked up the receiver.

'You're in danger! I beg you, I plead with you, come today, I have to talk to you. You're in danger! I beg you, come to 6 Danko Street, at four o'clock this afternoon. Come, I implore you. Your life's at stake.' After whispering these words, Regina rang off.

'A wrong number! At this hour of the morning!' murmured Lia. 'People are awful!' She turned over and went back to sleep.

Abramo Fleischmann couldn't get to sleep again. 'Danger? What danger? The ravings of a lunatic! Just imagine!' And yet he felt uneasy. Strangely, this girl didn't say generic things, quite the reverse. On the other hand, perhaps the danger did exist. For an hour he thought only of that. At six o'clock the phone rang again.

'You answer, please. If it's a nuisance caller, tell them to clear off!' whispered Abramo Fleischmann. His wife picked up the receiver.

So it was that the professor learned from his wife's mouth of the discovery of the protein Hox A91, the one controlling the differentiation of the cells that form the head of every animal. The head! The brain! The mind!

Abramo Fleischmann shouted with joy, leaped out of bed, ran to the kitchen, to the bathroom, walked the length of his apartment, unable to stay still or contain his own joy. Then he shut himself in the shoe cupboard, threw himself on the floor and began sobbing.

His life's work was accomplished. Certainly the most prestigious prizes, the greatest awards would be heaped upon him. He could consider himself the father and creator of the future of humanity.

He stood up. He went back to the bathroom and washed his face. In a not too far-off future they would even be able to bring someone who had been beheaded back to life!

He felt taller, straighter. A balanced, wise and benevolent creature dwelt in his body. The ceiling was lower: Lia, too, struck him as more graceful, more worthy of compassion. He dressed in a hurry and went out into the dawn, walking to the Institute. Bottles of wine, fresh cakes and coffee awaited him, an uncontainable euphoria had spread among his fellow workers, who were hugging and kissing as they arrived at work.

At nine in the morning the phone rang and when the professor picked it up to give the minister the news, he heard only Regina's voice, which whispered to him five, six, ten times: 'You have to come and find me! Right away! Right away! I'm ill. I'm very ill. I'm about to die.'

'There's always some loser throwing her own shame in your face. But isn't it possible to enjoy the beauty of creation in peace?' thought the furious Professor Fleischmann. He didn't consider for a second the possibility that the girl might be in danger. The phone rang again, and when he answered he didn't hear a voice, merely the faint crackling of the blocked line. The same thing happened twice more in the space of two minutes.

'Some anonymous trouble-maker. Please, you answer from now on,' he said to his secretary. Regina might have been lying bleeding, poisoned, suffocated. He didn't care. He had things to do, he had won, and he had to enjoy his victory in peace. The whole day was spent in feverish consultations: how to give the news to the world, which foreign colleague to tell first, the patent, the minister, the experiments that would now have to be set up, the finances to be sought. That evening he had some friends over and Lia cooked an excellent Spanish dinner. At midnight another three calls came, followed by silence.

'Have you got a secret lover?' asked Lia, halfway between serious and joking. Fleischmann's friends were refilling their glasses.

'Last week I saw him with a beautiful blonde,' said his closest colleague, Dr Kupfer.

Professor Fleischmann joined in the joke and said he knew five blondes. And dark colours were forbidden in his harem. Redheads at most were allowed in.

Fleischmann went to bed happy.

'I never thought I would live through a day like that. Everything on earth used to have a meaning: good and evil, beauty and ugliness. It's coming back,' he said to Lia when the last guest had gone.

'We'll have to find a cure for Alzheimer's. It isn't right that old age should hold that disintegration in store for so many human beings,' murmured Lia.

'The ruin of the old precedes the construction of the new,' said Fleischmann. Then he wondered where he had come across that sentence. After a moment he remembered Regina. 'She said it to me!' he thought. 'Poor thing! May she rest in peace.' Within himself he had killed and buried her.

But the next day, and for the rest of the week, the phone rang at five in the morning, and then again in the office at nine o'clock precisely, and no one at the other end said a word.

'You've got to call the police!' said Lia. 'Call the police! It's impossible to bear persecution like this. I know there are unbalanced people who are devoted to that kind of practical joke. We've got to find out who's been calling every day and resolve the situation once and for all.'

Professor Fleischmann contacted the district chief of police, Marshal H.

'Are you sure you want us to intervene, Professor!' asked the marshal from behind his pitiful desk.

'Yes,' answered Fleischmann.

'Are you aware of the fact that we will record all of your conversations and listen to the material recorded every day? You won't have a moment's privacy.'

'Really? Aren't there any other methods you could use? Couldn't you only check at certain times of day . . .?'

'No. If you want our help, that's the only method we've got. Maybe you're worried that we'll discover some irregularities, some secrets? We might well have discovered them already,' the marshal said rather coarsely. Then his attitude changed. 'Do you have any suspects?' he asked.

To reveal his own suspicions like that, his own certainties, would have meant revealing the secret of Regina. The professor abandoned his suggestion and realized that if he aroused the suspicions of the police, they would be sure to scrutinize his life from now on.

'I'll take the phone off the hook at night,' he said. 'I'm sorry to have bothered you.'

'Well, we're grateful for the information,' the marshal replied, an ambiguous smile on his lips.

By taking the phone off the hook every evening, and filtering calls to his office through his secretary, Abramo Fleischmann managed to free himself from his tormentor, and enjoyed a few weeks of great contentment, almost happiness. Everything was for the best, as though the universe had recovered its harmony.

In the spring there came the time of the genetic engineering conference that Fleischmann organized each year in a lakeside resort: he would meet up with old friends from all over the world, new ideas would celebrate the greatness of the human spirit. Lia, too, was preparing to leave for a conference in Florence.

'Sorry I can't witness your triumph. But you know I'm

with you anyway,' she said one evening in bed before giving him a kiss and putting out the light. For Professor Fleischmann life was keeping its promises. As if the disaster in which his family had died was the price to pay for future happiness: for his definitive self-realization, for his new maturity as a man.

The long-awaited day arrived. At the end of the car journey, after stopping to refresh himself in the little apartment that was placed at his disposal, Fleischmann finally entered the large hall crammed full of academics. From his pocket he drew his speech, with which he would announce his discovery, and was already about to begin reading when his eye fell on a guest sitting in the front row: her hair held back with a coloured scarf, very smartly dressed. Regina greeted him with a smile.

'What's she doing here? How did she manage to get herself invited? What trick can she have dreamed up?' Fleischmann speculated. Then he put on his glasses and started reading with a firm voice and a cheerful solemnity. He couldn't stop his glance, as it roamed at random from the chosen speakers to the guests, from constantly returning to Regina as if under a spell. By the end he felt as though he had read the speech for her alone.

There was a good deal of applause, genuine ovations, everyone thronged around him, hugged him, kissed him. Regina approached as well, threw her arms around his neck and whispered to him: 'You know you were waiting for me. Now we've found each other.'

She pulled away from him and disappeared.

Throughout the rest of the day, which he spent reading reports, delivering commemorative speeches, making greetings and taking refreshments, the girl didn't appear again. Late in the evening, on the point of going to sleep, Abramo Fleischmann heard a knock at the door of the outbuilding of the castle in which he had stayed regularly for fifteen years when conferences were on. All of a sudden he remembered Regina. He said 'Who is it?' too brusquely: after all, it could have been the secretary, or the chambermaid. There was no reply. He stayed listening in silence, but no one spoke. Instead the knocking came again, louder and longer this time.

'Come on, who is it?' asked Fleischmann, decidedly flustered. Again there was no reply, just the same loud and insistent noise. Keen to avoid scandal, he decided to open up. As he was making his way towards the door, he didn't assume any attitude in particular. He didn't know what to show: indignation, anger, indifference or nothing at all. He opened the door.

Regina was there in the half-darkness, and only when she came towards him, with a slow and indecisive step, did the professor discern her face bathed with tears, and hear her subdued sobbing.

'We've found each other. We've found each other,' she whispered. She held out her hand, and all that Fleischmann could do was shake it, as if in an official greeting.

Then he launched in, roughly, convinced of being in the right: 'Why have you been phoning at dawn like that? Do you want to ruin my life, throw me into chaos?'

'I didn't do anything. Why are you accusing me of such awful things?'

'Haven't you been calling me for weeks and weeks, at five in the morning? Waking up the whole house, my wife who does a difficult job and needs her sleep?'

'No, it wasn't me.'

A terrible rage seized Fleischmann.

'So you dare to deny it, you wretch? Go away, leave me in peace, I don't even know who you are, I don't know your name, I don't know what you do. You're destruction personified, you're gangrene. Clear off!'

Regina started crying more loudly than before.

'No, all I want is what's good for you. I'm not capable of harming anyone, I'm ill, rejected by one and all, they beat me, despise me, they only throw me out because I'm not capable of doing any harm. Come back to yourself, accept my love, I ask nothing in return, nothing at all, I don't want to cause you any trouble. Just think that if you want to live in goodness, all of you has to be there, evil will be contented with just a little bit. Please, think about it. I implore you!'

She threw her arms around his neck and Fleischmann felt her hot tears running down to his shoulders, under his shirt. He was impressed.

'All right, come in,' he said in a low voice, shaking off

Regina's desperate embrace with some difficulty, leaning against the wall which was papered with a rustic pattern.

Regina took out some paper handkerchiefs and dried her face. She was, as usual, dressed entirely in grey clothes, now a little threadbare.

They said nothing for a few moments. Then Fleischmann started talking quietly. 'You're a good person. I want to help you. I don't think you mean to hurt me. Or perhaps you don't even realize you're doing it?'

'No. I swear I'm not. I've dreamed of this moment for so long. Being able to talk to you like this, in peace; that was all I wanted. And now it's becoming a reality.'

'What do you want to talk about?' Fleischmann asked gently, as gently as possible. He hoped the whole embarrassing situation would come to an end soon, with a few well-chosen words.

'I want to talk to you about my youth, my tenderness, my love.'

'No, please. It's a subject I know nothing about. What are you referring to? I've never been in a relationship with you. I barely know you.'

Fleischmann was convinced that he was talking to a half-wit, who would accept his version of reality as he cared to present it.

'I know you barely know me. Just as you know nothing of me, of my suffering, of my humiliations, of my voice. I've kept on taking lessons, and now I can sing

53

very well. Do you want to hear the 'Lamentations for the Ruin of Jerusalem'? I'm more derelict than the city. But I'm not lamenting the fact. If you want to help me, fine, otherwise it doesn't matter. But take care of yourself. You've grown cynical, selfish, lying. You've become very wicked.'

'Please stop it,' Fleischmann said calmly. But the girl started crying again.

'You're not interested in anything, you live with your wife as if she were a piece of old meat. You sleep with her as you would with a leg of lamb.' Regina smiled between her tears. 'Isn't that how it is?'

'No,' Fleischmann replied uncertainly, but with a certain dignity.

'Have you ever wondered what she needs? What I need? Have you ever wondered what men need?'

'Please . . . although you do say intelligent things, I don't think you're a storehouse of truth.'

'Truth . . . You shouldn't even utter the word. You aren't in search of it. You hate it. And science, too, isn't in search of truth any more, just the possibility of going onwards, onwards, onwards towards the void.' Regina stopped crying. From her handbag she took the last paper handkerchief and blew her nose. Neither of them said anything.

All of a sudden the girl ran towards the sofa, threw herself on her knees and pressed herself to Abramo, whispering without drawing breath: 'Take me, I love you,

I love you, I want nothing from you. Embrace me, come inside me, please, please.' Drawing herself up, she started to kiss him on the mouth, on the neck, on the eyes, murmuring words filled with tenderness.

Professor Fleischmann had a brilliant intuition. If he pleasured the girl, giving her his mediocre love, the poor thing's obsession would be extinguished, satisfied once and for all.

He responded to her kisses, pressed her to him, told her to take off her clothes and began to undress in his turn, with meticulous slowness, while Regina, in a moment, threw herself on him again, naked, kissing him, licking him, stroking him.

'Come, come inside me, I've been waiting for you for so long.'

Fleischmann wanted to indicate the areas of his own body that he wanted her to touch, but she clasped him with her arms and legs.

'Here I am, I'm yours, all yours, you're inside me, you're my body,' she murmured.

He performed all the usual movements, she tried to kiss him, but his mind was only on completing, in the shortest possible time, the act of intercourse that he so little desired. He fished around in his mind for all his most exciting memories; he was really making love, as one celebrated scientist has put it, not with Regina, but with his own brain. Regina, on the other hand, seemed at the peak of passion, her body thrashed, her hands gripped

Abramo's flesh, with love and sweetness. It was all simply distressing for the professor. Regina began to groan, to twist and roar.

'Hug me! Hug me! Quickly! Hug me, like I've told you to!' Regina screamed at one point, and for Fleischmann it was like a lash from a whip. He flew into a raging frenzy.

He pulled away from her and in his turn began to yell, but with a muffled voice so that no one could hear him: 'What? You're giving me orders now? Go away, go away, you beast! Go away from here, clear off and never let me see you again. Go away, do you understand?'

It is painful to say this, but Fleischmann, formerly the mild-mannered scholar, began to slap the girl with all his strength, and when she defended herself by covering her face with her hands, he used his fists to beat her spine, her head and her floundering arms. 'Get dressed and go! Go away! I don't want to know anything about you, about your love, about your misery, about your phone-calls, about your silence! Go to hell!'

Regina tried to escape, but he followed her all around the room, like an unchained beast.

When Professor Fleischmann had stopped raining his blows upon her, without saying a word, her face red from his slaps, her arms and her neck covered with bruises, gasping for breath, Regina hurriedly dressed, walked towards the door, opened it and only asked, very gently: 'Do you realize what you've done?' She waited, panting, for a moment, and not receiving a reply she went away.

Fleischmann ran to the door, opened it again with a frenetic gesture and whispered: 'Come here! Come here immediately! Come back!' But Regina had already disappeared.

3

What we now call 'self-esteem' vanished forever from Abramo Fleischmann's soul. The celebrations did nothing to reassure him. The conference was to last a week, and by the second day Abramo wanted to flee. But where to? Fleeing himself, leaving himself in the street and living an anonymous, neutral existence was not possible. He had to bear all the evil that he contained within himself.

The following evening he heard another knock at the door. He knew that he was not capable of fighting off Regina's love. He decided not to open the door. He held his breath so that his presence in the room would not be heard. But the knocking continued and Kupfer appeared at the attic room window. 'Who is it?' he asked in the darkness.

Then Fleischmann opened the window and said: 'I've asked for a hot drink to be sent up. I was having a shower and didn't hear it. I'm sorry.'

'No, I'm sorry, professor. I didn't wish to interfere . . .
I'm sorry. I'm sorry . . .'

He would have gone on apologizing all night if
Fleischmann hadn't told him to go to sleep. The following
day it was his turn to tell the whole story of their discovery.

So Abramo had to open the door. Regina came in and
sat down on the sofa. She was wearing her dark clothes.
For a few minutes she didn't look at him, and
Fleischmann didn't have the courage to sit down opposite
her: it would have been like the Last Judgement.

'How can I help you? Tell me something,' he said in a
soft voice after a while.

Regina didn't reply. She sat with her head bowed. She
looked very beautiful. He had another 'brilliant' idea.

'I've been thinking about you all day. I've got some
money together. You can live on it for three or four
months if you want. It'll be enough for your singing
master. Here it is.'

He took from his wallet all the money he had brought
with him. Regina didn't move.

'All right, I'll put it here on the table,' said
Fleischmann, thinking himself suddenly on the side of
reason and equity.

'I don't want it,' Regina whispered. 'Do you realize
what you've done?'

Fleischmann was repelled by violence, but it didn't
seem to him that the world had collapsed after what he
had done the evening before . . . Yet it was so.

'All wickedness destroys the whole universe. And me, too.' Regina started sobbing softly. Then she went on. 'You still have time. But you will have to think seriously about who you are, about what you want. You will have to think about it. Day and night. Otherwise you're lost.' Now she was weeping more loudly, disconsolately.

'Take the money,' Professor Fleischmann said forcefully. 'It'll be useful to you. You're destroying yourself, too.'

Regina shook her head in a gesture of denial.

'Take it, I tell you,' whispered Abramo threateningly.

'I don't want anything from you until you're as I've said you should be. I haven't eaten for two days, but I want nothing from you. My brothers reject me, no one helps me, they all send me away, they want to lock me up in an institution. You want to send me away as well. You don't want to help me either.'

'But I do!' yelled Fleischmann. 'Take the money this minute! Take it!'

He grabbed Regina by her hair, pulled her to her feet and dragged her towards the table.

'Take the money!' he yelled again, shaking the girl repeatedly.

'What are you doing? Let me go! What are you trying to do?' shrieked Regina.

'This! This, this, this!' hissed Abramo, trying to force into Regina's open mouth the banknotes he had picked up from the table. Then all of a sudden he came to his senses. He threw himself face down on the sofa and began to cry. What should have been the finest moment of his life had hurtled into the abyss of abjection.

'I was trying to do something for you. I failed. A shame,' Regina said quietly. She took all the money, put it in her purse and went out into the night. Abramo opened the window and looked out after her. He hadn't remembered her being so beautiful and harmonious. He went into the bathroom. He saw himself in the mirror, with his mouth twisted downwards like a crying child.

'It's true,' he said out loud. 'Everything is being destroyed. Why? Why?'

His assistant's speech, the festivities, the vague allusion by the Swedish delegate to the greatest award in the world stunned Fleischmann, made him forget everything. He felt a kind of happiness barely veiled by the knowledge of himself and the evil that was hunting him down.

Regina appeared in the circle of people complimenting him for his brilliant research. She held out her hand and murmured with a smile: 'The money you gave me wasn't enough, unfortunately. I would need twice as much to pay my debts. I'm coming to your house this evening.' She pressed his hand again, warmly, and then her place was taken by academics and researchers coming to congratulate the professor. They headed towards the hall, where a magnificent dinner in his honour was waiting for them.

Late that evening he was attacked by violent stomach cramps. He hadn't emptied his bowels for at least six days: the stress of always, always, always doing something had made him forget those basic needs. He was familiar with the symptoms: when he reached a crucial point in his own life everything stopped, his guts wanted to store his waste, to close up inside themselves. He resolved to change that situation at all costs, he was prepared to bleed. He locked himself in the lavatory and tried to free himself from everything: he summoned all his energies as though it was a matter of life and death. There was a knock at the door.

'No!' exclaimed the professor. 'No!'

He continued with his own efforts. There was another knock, louder this time, and louder. Fleischmann could not even shout 'I'm coming', and the knocking was turning into thunder, or at least that was how it sounded to him. A thunder that distracted him from himself, imposed upon him another terror, another hypocrisy. Abraham was afraid of being discovered, of ending up 'on everyone's lips'. The knocking had now become unbearable.

'Even here, even now!' cried Fleischmann. 'You don't want to let me live, you want to destroy me whatever the cost!' He leapt to his feet, pulled up his trousers, and, holding them with one hand, went to open the door. He almost tore it from its hinges in his ardour.

'What do you want this time?' he hissed.

'Don't be like this. Let me in,' whispered Regina.

'No! You're never coming in here again! You're not coming into my life!'

'For one moment, just one moment, suspend your wickedness, your selfishness!'

Regina tried to climb the four steps leading to the door, and then Abramo started aiming mad blows at the girl's stomach, chest and face.

'No! You're not coming here again! Take your money and go!' He threw her some banknotes that he had withdrawn that afternoon. 'Go! Go away for ever. Monster!' Striking Regina in the face with all his strength, so that she fell to the floor covered in blood, Fleischmann didn't even notice that his trousers had fallen down, and that he was half-naked.

'That's what you are. Like all men. A bag of crap. Look at you,' gasped Regina. Abramo realized he was covered in excrement.

'You'll regret all this. But it'll be too late. It's too late even now.' Regina started to cry. 'I'm sorry for you. I'd have liked to have done something to save you. You wouldn't let me. Now you're finished.'

'I've given you money,' Fleischmann murmured.

'Money?' Regina said in a barely audible voice. 'Keep it, wipe your arse with your money!' She threw the banknotes on the floor and went down the stairs. Fleischmann heard the slam of the door and then stayed immersed in darkness.

'Professor, can I help you?' Kupfer said cautiously from the door of his attic.

The conclusion of the story of Abramo Fleischmann is bewildering. We have reconstructed it with the help of Kupfer. At the end of the conference Fleischmann couldn't go home in his car, because there was a problem with the engine. He took the train along with his secretary. At a certain point the door of the compartment opened and Regina appeared. She sat down opposite Fleischmann, showing her swollen and injured face.

'His visage was so marred more than any man, and his form more than the sons of men.' 52: 24.

'I've had a thrombosis in my legs. I'm going home to my brothers. They're no different from you, professor. They're no worse. Congratulations on your magnificent discoveries.' That was all Regina said. For two hours she displayed her martyred face, then disappeared into the crowd of the Southern Station.

One evening, some time later, Fleischmann, now close to receiving the Great Award, unexpectedly failed to come home. His wife looked for him in vain, the police couldn't find him even after months of searching. According to what the professor had confided to Dr Kupfer during those days, he had become fixated with the idea of finding Regina at all costs. Nothing else mattered to him, honour, knowledge, family and society no longer had any value in his eyes. He loved only the girl he had so violently sent away. The true conclusion?

According to some of his friends Abramo Fleischmann was seen in Benares, in India, in the headquarters of a Hindu sect; according to others in Jerusalem, at the foot of the Weeping Wall, as a beggar. Many articles were written in the papers, many programmes were made on television. His case is more mysterious than that of the scientist Majorana, who also disappeared, no one knows where or how. Some people claim to have seen Fleischmann, together with Regina, in the pitiful garden of a little half-derelict cottage in the district known as the Land of Angels.

If we are to lend credence to this version, we should believe the saying: 'Better an hour of repentance and good deeds in this world than all the life in the World to Come.'

But we should also consider the other saying: 'There is no suffering without iniquity.'

Some suggest that Fleischmann sought death in the Danube, and that his corpse was found in Romania, three weeks after his disappearance.

THE TWO ANGELS

Behold, I take away from thee the desire of
thine eyes with a stroke: yet neither shalt thou
mourn nor weep, neither shall thy tears run dry.

EZEKIEL 24: 16

Dear friend. You have turned up after forty years, asking
for news of me, to add me the list of your schoolmates
who are now largely established in their respective careers.
I don't think the book you're working on will be a volu-
minous one. Statistics on the success of those who grew
up among the less affluent classes, to which we ourselves
belonged, are not encouraging. But for myself, I may say
with some pride that I am now one of the richest men in
the whole of Australia. I know little about you. Since we
separated, I have visited the old continent only occasion-
ally, almost always staying in London, to sign a financial or
industrial contract. Over the past twenty years, it is true,
I have returned to my homeland more frequently, but
only to follow the progress of the illnesses of my dear relations, and then to bury them one after another. Can I

refer to these sad occasions as 'going back'? Would it not be better clearly to call them what they are: terrible blows of fate?

And as regards human destinies, since you have turned your attention to me after so many years, I am taking advantage of this to ask you a favour and offer you an opportunity. I have lost all trace of two people whose welfare is very close to my heart. I have written letters, sent telegrams, made very expensive money transfers to two private investigators in Melbourne, involved the authorities, but all in vain. The request that I would like to make to you, you who have stayed faithful to our homeland while I have come here, to this far-off land, is to go, if possible three times a week for a period of two months, to two addresses that I am sending you, and to check whether the windows of the houses that I am about to describe to you are illuminated at night, whether there is any sign of life, whether they are inhabited by the two people whose identities I shall now reveal to you. This is my first attempt. After that . . . I don't know what may happen after that.

The two dwellings in question are unfortunately some distance apart, in two districts that are far from one another: the eighth district and the first. For your expenses, should any arise, I can send you the sum required for the hire of a car (small capacity) and reimburse the cost of the petrol. Forgive the cheek, but if, as I sense from your letter, you are living 'decently', you are not wallowing in riches. A little supplementary income (three hundred dollars a week) might be useful to you.

Who are the people I wish to find? A lady of eighty-five, my great-aunt, and a girl of eleven, Eva, the daughter of a sociologist and a greengrocer at the market.

The first lives at number one St Stephen's Park, along the bank of the Danube. She resides, if she is still alive, in a two-room apartment. She survived the war and until a short time ago, although well on in years, she was still an example of good humour and vitality. Every day she did her shopping on her own, she read the papers, watched television, left the house to go and sit in the park with her friends, gossiping about the past and the future which flowed in her mind like the waves of the 'beautiful blue Danube' beyond the little park. I have had no news of her for seven months. I have called her many times, I have bothered her neighbours: without success. I wouldn't wish her to be dead in any place or any manner unknown to me. Murder and rape are on the rise in our country. It will seem strange, but I need her. Over the past few years I have gone to see her now and then, to draw from those visits the energy needed to face life's difficulties. Yes, that old lady's example fills me with courage. In your letter you ask me how, 'really', I have become rich. It is not easy to answer that, because to all appearances I have been a dishonest exploiter of people. That is not the reality. You remember my Susanna, my wonderful wife who left me a widower two years ago after a brief and dreadful illness (a brain tumour)? The idea that made me rich was hers. Susanna was very beautiful when we arrived here in Melbourne. Her blonde hair, her white and pink cheeks, her powerful hips, her beautiful legs were a sensation even here. I remember, when we were newly-weds, how you looked at her, you, the confirmed bachelor, when you came to see us that Sunday morning. We were usually loafing about in bed. She had no shame, she showed her body to everyone, but I alone was allowed to enjoy it. She was reserved, gentle. She was the one who suggested that I open a sex shop, practically a brothel, here in Melbourne. She ran it for five years. That business quickly enabled me to set aside a certain amount of capital. Again, it was she who drove me on to take the next step. I set up a contraceptive factory. My official biography has appeared in the major European magazines, there's no point in going into it at length and repeating it to you, you know everything. Now I have moved into the great telecommunications industry. And to think that I started out dealing with the most primitive form of communication, the one that occurs between one body and another. As I have already told you, at a certain point all the dear people I left behind in my homeland began to die. My mother, my father, my uncles and aunts. All I have left is that one last relative, my grandmother's sister. I am sending you her photograph as a girl, and one taken some years ago, so that you will be able to recognize her. As you see, she has changed little over the years. Look at her wonderful raven hair then, and how it looks today, obviously dyed! It's strong and soft, as it always was. And her expression! The same vivacious irony as before. You should hear her sing: she still has a lovely strong, supple, harmonious voice. How she sings the songs of the gypsies, and even some of today's pop songs! It's a joy to hear her. And, you won't believe it, but she still has the desire to live, to have fun, to enjoy, even if only in her imagination, the pleasures of sex. If there is an excuse, every now and again she pulls up her skirt to show off her legs. They are very soft, rather raw-looking but not disgusting. When I returned to my homeland to visit her, she used to prepare me a place beside her in the broad sofa-bed, and demanded that I sleep there because she was afraid of the dark. 'Don't snore,' she ordered, 'and keep your hands to yourself during the night, you understand?' she said before putting out the light. I felt sorry for her, I obeyed, I told myself again and again that I had to humour her, she had so little time left to live. After a minute I usually fell into the deepest sleep, but she stayed awake: she listened to a tiny radio that she pressed against her ear and followed the nightly broadcasts. She commented on them out loud, in words that would have made anyone blush.

She spoke loudly, growling the same sentence seven or eight times before moving on, bundling together different meanings and words: from her language she spouted chaos rather than order. There was no peace: her mind was constantly producing something which resembled a human discourse, but which was not. And so I would listen to her all night, because her ceaseless verbiage woke me up from time to time until I plunged back into unconsciousness, into the nothingness of sleep. I could have gone to luxurious hotels, I could have had the most beautiful girls in the city for company, and yet I would not have found the vital charge that that old woman exuded.

Our dear rabbi Stern had spoken to us so many times of the two angels: the one who walks ahead of us and the one who walks behind. Aunt Leila is the angel who comes in front of me. Her great round eyes move in every direction, examining, registering everything. She is the past that watches us, pitilessly. She has already settled her accounts with everything. She is calm, sceptical, her soul is in peace. But as far as I am concerned, she leaves me dangling in the present, like a hanged man who cannot die; I am suspended here, without any ground for my feet to rest on, my hands bound and, for all their terrible strength, unable to do anything, the air that neither leaves nor enters my lungs, my eyes bursting from their sockets, my feet kicking in the painful, dreadful nothingness of the present. Forgive my outburst, but as you will have sensed, I am desperate. I am suffering from a form of depression that no one can cure. But let us talk about the other angel.

This one is a girl of eleven.

I saw her a year ago, in a wretched block of flats to which I had returned after a long time, at number four Great Transport Street. As you will remember, immediately I had finished the eighth class, with considerable difficulty, I had set to some hard graft in Teleki Square market. In the morning I unloaded boxes of fruit, bags full of wood and coal, dismembered cows. In the afternoon, in a dark and stinking gymnasium, I queued up for all-in wrestling matches. After one particularly amusing match, a girl was waiting for me by the exit. Someone I didn't know. 'Come with me,' she said without any introduction. 'I like you. I'm not a whore. I like you, with all those muscles. I've always dreamed of a man like that.' For two years we made love in basements, in parks, among the bushes of the Cool Valley. One day she didn't come to our date. She had found an old textile merchant and married him.

After the death of my adored Susanna, I was gripped by a great sense of loneliness. I returned to my homeland and looked for my first girlfriend, in the house where she had been living when we first met. She was still living there. Her husband had died four years after their marriage. And their daughter, a sociologist's wife, had died of a tumour in the breast. All my former girlfriend had left was her little granddaughter. It was August. The granddaughter was wearing tight little pale green trousers and a bodice of the same colour which revealed her little

71

belly and her navel. Her hair was tied back into a pony-tail.

'Are you really famous?' she asked when her grand-mother introduced me.

'No,' I answered. 'I'm not famous. I'm very rich.'

'If you're rich, you're famous as well. Money and fame are everything,' she said gently. 'I want to be a writer, or an actress, or a billionaire.' She was standing in front of me, her steady blue eyes staring at me with cruel objectivity. A secret and inscrutable world radiated from that gaze. I always wear a gold bracelet around my wrist. My poor Susanna said it was a mark of vulgarity. I know that, too. But I don't know the difference between vulgarity and refinement. That day I slipped the bracelet off my wrist, showed it to the girl and gave it to her.

'Wear it in health and happiness,' I said.

Giving presents to Eva – that's the little girl's name – became my amusement. She received everything with indifference, her cruel expression didn't even interrogate me. Only the day I gave her a pearl necklace she asked me: 'Why are you giving me these presents?'

'I don't know,' I answered. 'I've been told that you're my angel. I want you to watch over me well.'

'Watch over you? I don't understand,' she said, before putting on the necklace. She was very beautiful, her breasts offered themselves to the touch, her throat to kisses. I gave her a silk dress, wonderful shoes that emphasized the beauty of her ankles, her tender legs. A pair of jewelled earrings was my final gift. Then I left, returning to my 'exotic' Australia, a country that waits to see where the world is going before it follows. Later, an irresistible longing, whether for Aunt Leila or for her, called me back to my dusty old homeland, my paradise lost. Last year I transferred part of my capital to a bank in our country. I bought an antique diadem – rubies, diamonds and pearls mounted on white gold. It came from Baghdad market. In Paris, for Aunt Leila, I bought perfumes and a Dior dress of white silk with flowers embroidered in gold. When I caught the plane, my secretary handed me the packages and I set off. When I arrived, after a nine-hour flight, I immediately took a taxi to the district where Eva lived with her grandmother. Outside the wretched apartment block I paid the driver and climbed the stairs with my heart in my mouth. I wanted to see whether my angel's glacial indifference would finally have changed into an expression of joy. I wanted her for myself, I wanted to marry her. I knocked at the door, but no one answered. I knocked again, and again, now beginning to panic. I was like a man about to drown who, his lungs full of water, slowly moves his arms and legs, neither living nor dying, condemned to stay suspended in the infinite water for all eternity. A toothless old man poked his head out of a door and mumbled to me that the two women – grandmother and granddaughter – hadn't been seen for about a month. But he knew that they came back sometimes, at night, to get something and disappear again. Perhaps they were living at the home of a 'friend' of the girl, who had recently picked up some bad habits. She would send her grandmother out and receive visits from youths and elderly men, their laughter and shouts of pleasure echoing around the whole block. An outrage.

'My angel, the angel who follows in my footsteps!' I thought. The neighbour added, 'Two or three visits every day. Sometimes she would lean out of the window, inviting people in the street to come up and join her. Unsavoury people, drunks.' He shook his head for a long time, with his eyes fixed on the ground because of his curved spine. Then he said goodbye to me and, with a slow and complicated manoeuvre, he turned back into his tiny apartment.

I went down the stairs. I was frightened, carrying those precious parcels. On Wednesday Street I quickened my pace. By now it was beginning to get dark. On the Corner of Teleki Square I found a taxi, got in and told the very fat and asthmatic driver to take me to St Stephen's Park. If there was no future, I would seek shelter in the past. I climbed the stairs, anticipating Aunt Leila's joy as she received the finest presents of her life: I could almost smell her cheap perfume, which I would replace with my Chanel No. 19. I would also give her the diadem meant for Eva. All the bitterness of the child's flight would be transformed into happiness. As you may imagine, I didn't find Aunt Leila either. I knocked for ten minutes. 'She's deaf, the poor thing, it'll be a while before she hears me,' I thought. But nonetheless it was already evening, my aunt was not at home. Instead, behind the curtain of her glass door there appeared her eighty-five-year-old neighbour, Aunt Matthew, as everyone called her because of her little white beard. With a nod she beckoned me to the door and invited me into the one pretty little room. In five minutes she told me that to the great disapproval of the whole building, my aunt had for months been receiving visits from an eighteen-year-old boy, a distant relation. They had become inseparable 'friends'. The boy visited her every day after school, before going home, lest his parents become suspicious and forbade the boy to frequent the strange old woman. Then the boy stopped coming. And Aunt Leila disappeared as well. No one knew who to tell, who to turn to. Perhaps she would come back one day. Someone said they had seen her, in the evening, wandering along the corridors inside the building. Maybe it was a ghost. Every now and again the lights went on, and then it was dark again.

That's the story of the angel who walks ahead of me and the one who follows behind. They have both disappeared. Now I'm really alone, with my wealth . . . with my present. That's why I beg you to do me this last favour. I can't give up, I want to find those two people, whose addresses I am sending you on the enclosed card, along with my new address. For two months I have been in a clinic in Melbourne. If you want to come and see me, book the plane ticket in my name. That's what fame and money are for, when the angels have disappeared. To try not to die alone like a dog.

Yours, N. G.

VICTIM AND MURDERER

> Charity frees us from death, not only from
> violent death, but from death itself.

SHAB. 156B.

Dear Doctor

You will forgive me if, in replying to your letter, I don't
use the familiar form of address as I did at school, but so
many years have passed. You have had a reasonable career,
while I have lagged behind, terribly far behind. For that
reason I am turning to you with all due deference. The
experience that I am about to relate to you has marked my
life, as the great events of history do to those who live
through them. The facts in question go back ten years, and
yet I cannot help remembering, every day, the images and
the terrible impressions that those hours have left me with.
I have spent all this time deciding to talk about them, but
after living through the events that I want to illustrate to
you, making even a tiny decision is a great effort for me.

Before I begin, a very brief introduction.

Ten years ago, after a long illness, I lost my twin brother, the person I loved most in the world. Of course I hadn't loved him just because, from the genetic point of view at least, he was like me: my solipsism never took me to such extremes. I loved him because I had never met anyone with his gentle nature, his fine and ready intelligence, his sensitivity to other people's problems and his dignity, always firm but never ostentatious. His illness was long but not cruel. Apart from the last two or three weeks it treated him with clemency, but remained irreversible. Death by cardiac arrest, caused by the lack of oxygen in the blood, came very quickly. A great crowd came to the funeral: friends, patients, relations. No one wept for him theatrically: his memory aroused the same discretion and silent benevolence that radiated from his character. I myself, for weeks and months, felt as though I was someone else, less of a liar, less violent, better disposed towards my fellow men. I can't understand what can have distinguished us in that way over the course of the years.

Finally, I had a long and painful discussion with Rabbi Feldstein, about the uniqueness or otherwise of the soul of twins. 'The soul descends to us the second day after conception,' said Feldstein, and to my great amazement he referred to the Book of Ruth, which is perhaps the most precious gem in the celebrated *Book of Splendour*. Unable to compete with him on this terrain, I referred more modestly to recent studies in genetics. 'You'd be better off reading the conclusions of Dr Crick, and you'll see that in the end everything will sort itself out in your mind according to the steps shown in the Book of Ruth,' said the rabbi. 'Science, even when it leads to practical results, is merely a metaphor for a higher wisdom. Beware of taking it at face value!'

I fled in horror from the house of that learned man. To rely on science in that kind of spirit seemed to me to be the fruit of a childish mentality.

During those first weeks of struggle, I organized my days so that I could go to my brother's grave, returning, with his memory, to the time of our childhood, when lies and fiction had not yet become a part of me, when I had not yet been overwhelmed. 'How did it all happen?' I wondered. 'Why do I have to bear that damnation? Why did Cain and Abel have to become what they did: victim and murderer? Who will answer me that question?' Oh, there are answers, but as an adult I can't accept them. And so, throughout those days, I continued to ask myself questions, to return, with my visits to the cemetery and through hypnosis, ever further into the past. Dr Schmidt, who had carried out countless experiments with the dancers of the Opera House, took me on for his memory exercises. (The dancers were the only people to engage for free in the first tests carried out by the man who is now a famous neuropsychiatrist.) According to the proponents of biochemistry, as you know, hypnosis is considered a superficial and harmful medium, but the joy

I felt in remembering, syllable by syllable, essays I had written in class at the age of seven, and phrases that I had copied without restraint from my brother, was certainly not a superficial feeling.

One October afternoon, leaving the office of the import–export company where I worked, I climbed into my Volvo and went to the old cemetery on the Pilgrims' Way. I drove along the tree-lined avenues, and walked to plot H, towards the fresh mound, still covered with flowers, of my beloved twin. All of a sudden, on the ground, I noticed something that I could not at first identify. A moment later, at the edge of the avenue, between the asphalt and the flowerbeds of the graves, I saw the motionless body of a tiny kitten, perhaps newly born. I went over to stroke it and discovered to my horror that the kitten's skull had been smashed: there was a drop of blood on that little head abandoned on the ground. A little way off a human figure was moving quickly away between the trees and the bushes. I recognized the workman whose duty it was to tend to the graves: a gipsy who would do any job for a tip. He was conscientious and punctual, but he also added personal touches of his own, a flower on the stones, water changed scrupulously in the vases, a pebble to testify to the dead person that he himself had been there. He had a spade over his shoulder. Clearly it had been he who had beaten that innocent little creature. Rather than drowning it, as was the custom among the peasants, he had reserved for it that horrendous death. I wanted to catch up with him and ask him the reason for his cruel action, but I stopped myself. A little further off there was the monument to the martyrs of the Second World War, who had died in the gas chambers. How could one ask the reason for their deaths, and whom would one ask? That monument also recalled innocent children suffocated with cyanide, frail women, defenceless men: who allowed all that to happen? I abandoned my intention and went on my way. A few steps further on, I noticed two more kittens on the asphalt with their heads smashed in. 'Damn you!' I murmured to myself, but the next moment I retracted the curse, or at least I tried to: words and events can't be 'retracted', curses resound for eternity, you can't create a situation in which they were never uttered or thought, whereby events never happened. I was sorry to have let such a thought enter my head and solemnly promised myself that I would somehow make reparation for my wickedness as well as for the grave-keeper's violence. I walked on. All around there could be heard the cheerful chatter of sparrows, I detected the harmonious whistling of a thrush. I caught sight of my brother's grave and felt a pang of joy, as though I was really going to meet him, to talk to him, as so often, of interesting and serious matters. Tears came to my eyes. 'My little one!' I cried silently, seeing in my mind's eye the calm face, the sweet and ironic expression of my brother as an adolescent. A moment later I suddenly stopped. On the ground, in the middle of the path, as though to obstruct my way, was the body of a fourth kitten. The gipsy had left it there! Without even the sense of pity to put it on the edge of the path! As if life equalled nothing, as though it could be treated on a par with garbage, with a pile of rubbish! I was about to utter a second curse but I managed to restrain myself. I went over to the poor creature, to push it to the edge of the road with my foot. At that point I noticed with horror that the kitten was still alive, breathing with difficulty, while a column of ants was already heading towards its mouth and its eyes.

'I can't let it die like this!' I thought. 'I can't! I'm responsible for its life, for its suffering. I must help it!' I looked around. There was no one in the cemetery apart from that executioner, who was hiding somewhere or other. Just like our own Grim Reaper, who lies in wait throughout our whole lives, among the trees, behind the wardrobe, under the bed, in our brains.

What was I to do? I didn't dare touch its body, probably infected with who knows what foul micro-organisms, bacilli, viruses, fungi. I put my hat on the ground and pushed in the kitten's stiffened body with my foot. Its mouth was half-closed, it clenched its teeth as though clinging to life. There was no time to lose. If I wanted to alleviate its few remaining moments, I would have to run, buy some milk, pour it down its throat and keep it warm, close to the radiator, so that the first cold of that autumn didn't make its passing even more dreadful. In my heart I asked my brother's forgiveness and hurried towards the exit of the cemetery, pressing my loden hat to my chest. I carefully opened the car door: any abrupt movement might create a terrible shock for that tiny creature that had been beaten to death. I set it down on the back seat and started the engine.

In the first bar I found along the road I bought half a litre of milk and rushed home. As I drove the car, every now and again I looked at the little creature laid out on the back seat; it was still breathing, with difficulty, desperately. Its mouth half closed, its clenched teeth gave its face an evil, almost devilish expression. It communicated nothing, and yet with its desperate existence it said everything. I parked the car just below the house, ignoring the parking restrictions. I picked up the kitten and ran up the stairs. No one saw me. I opened the door with difficulty, and without even shutting it behind me I went into the kitchen where I put the little creature on the floor on a dry rag, beside the warm radiator. I poured the milk into a cup and tried to pour it into the mouth of the dying kitten, as I would have done for a human being. The kitten's teeth were still clenched and I tried to force them open with the spoon, but to no avail. The milk ran onto the floor, beside the little head laid on its left side.

I didn't give up and began gently to rub the little creature's mouth with the rim of the spoon. The kitten's desperate bite yielded imperceptibly and I was able to pour the milk into that tormented little body. I waited for the beneficial effects of the warm liquid. Apparently there

were none, because the kitten didn't move, even clench-
ing its teeth again to bite, a wild obstinacy, what remained
of its life. It was three o'clock in the afternoon, it was
beginning to get dark and I had to dash to the office. I
would have liked to have stayed close to the kitten, assur-
ing it of my presence, keeping it company throughout
those terrible moments. But did it know, that tiny creature, what its fate would be? Did it sense the closeness of
the end? Or did it perhaps lack that instinct that has been
described so often? I looked at it and, seized by great
pity, I began to stroke it without fear of contagion or
infection. I stroked it for a few seconds, but even that had
no effect: it didn't even close its eyes, as cats do when you
stroke them. Then I decided to detach myself from it:
what I was doing was insane. The ancient mechanisms
that governed life were stronger than my pity. Soon the
kitten would be dead, as billions upon billions of creatures
before it had died, since the first living cell had begun to
function on earth.

I went out. I was furious to discover that the city police
had had my car towed away. I was going to waste half a
day getting it back. 'There you are, that's what my stupid
sentimentalism has cost me. I'm not going to be the one
to interrupt the infinite chain of births and deaths. Why
am I wearing myself out like this, to correct the cruelty of
existence?' I said out loud.

I called the office, invented some excuse to explain
my absence and got on a bus to go and collect the car.

During that long journey I recalled the muzzle of the kitten, stiff with paralysis. The effort of its breath, the dying animal's desperate bite filled me with a kind of anguished terror. I identified with that kitten, as I would have done out of pity for any animal or human being. That kitten asked for nothing, it wasn't even capable of doing so; and yet I heard something like a universal cry for help issuing from its little mouth. Language isn't the only thing that counts, there's something beyond language that communicates a great deal more. In the beginning was not the word, but being.

Once I had got the bureaucratic chores out of the way, I finally regained possession of the vehicle for which I had no particular love, but which I needed for my work. I set off for home. As I got out, I noticed a stain of blood and greenish excrement on the back seat. I could never get it cleaned now: that horrible stain had ruined the fabric. I would either have to have the seat replaced or keep by me, until I sold the car, the mark of the kitten's desperate agony and death. Death and the degrading dirt which precedes and accompanies it, excrement and blood would boil up in me for ever, entering my brain, my imagination. That cat was putting its mark on me for the rest of my life. And yet I set off homewards anyway. I felt a duty to help as best I could that creature that had been beaten to death, simply because it was in the world, as I was. Having parked the car and covered the seat with a newspaper, I climbed the stairs two by two. I hoped with all my heart that the kitten would still be alive. I opened the door with some difficulty, my hands trembling. I went inside and immediately headed for the kitchen, looking at the place where I had laid the kitten, near the radiator. I heard a weak sound coming from its mouth, a harrowing and irrevocable miaow: the kitten was calling me. It was alive, it was calling for my help. 'There you are, life is stronger than all my doubts,' I thought. 'It isn't so easy to defeat, not even the most sinister of murderers can conquer it.'

I warmed up a little milk again, crouched down by the little animal and began to feed it. Its jaws were less stiff, and I managed to get a bit of liquid into its little mouth. For a moment it seemed to me that the kitten was closing its eyes, as if relieved of the torment of agony, at peace with death. 'My little one,' I said quietly. 'You see, I didn't leave you alone.'

At that moment the shrill ringing of the telephone shattered our profound and intimate communication. The sound struck me like a whiplash, my muscles contracted, I gave a start and saw that the kitten, although paralysed, was reacting too.

I silently excused myself and went to answer it. It was Ruth, the woman with whom I had been involved in a long and stormy friendship. She had been living in the town of Cinque Chiese for about a year, and now she wanted to see me.

'Come on,' she whispered, 'I feel like being with you, we haven't seen each other for three weeks now.'

I loved that woman with her childish manner of talking, her kind and expansive ways: her intimate, passionate goodness mixed with a naïve and smiling tenderness held me in thrall. Every time I was with her I regained my trust in myself and in life. 'What have I done to deserve this gift?' I wondered. Nonetheless I was incapable of being with her: my very passion for her frightened me and advised me to choose other outlets for my emotional life.

That afternoon, hearing her on the telephone, I too felt a very strong desire to see her again. But what to do with the kitten in its death throes? Take it with me on the train? And what if it died on the journey, how would I get rid of that filthy little corpse?

I could have entrusted the poor little thing to someone. But to whom? These doubts flashed around my head in a moment. 'What should I do?' I asked.

'Don't you know how to get to my place?' Ruth answered, and I heard a hint of perplexity in her voice.

'No, it's not that,' I said. 'There's an obstacle. A little obstacle.'

'Obstacle? What obstacle?' Ruth asked with harrowing regret. 'Are there obstacles between us now?'

'No,' I answered. And in a single breath I told her the story of the kitten. For a moment she remained silent. Then, in no uncertain terms, she told me to stay where I was. The dying creature needed me: she could wait. In conclusion she added, 'This isn't just a story you've made up so as not to see me?'

'No. I swear it isn't,' I hurried to reassure her. 'Or rather, I can't wait for . . .'

'No! I beg you! Don't wish for the death of that poor kitten. Never wish for the death of anyone or anything. Don't you know that death is evil? All the sacred texts say so.'

I hesitated. I felt slightly embarrassed opposite the object of my love, the woman who had read the sacred books while I settled for that one by Professor Crick.

'Fine. I'll stay here. But couldn't you come to me?'

'I can't. I have three patients here. I can't leave them.' Ruth was a nurse, and took her work very seriously.

It seemed to me to be going too far, all in all, to give such importance to the death of a kitten compared to three human lives. At that moment the cat's desperate little voice was heard in the darkness. It called out two or three times and then fell silent. The sound was incredibly sharp and penetrating: disarmed, defenceless against evil, it was the voice of pity that echoed through my house.

'Did you hear it?' I asked Ruth.

'No, I didn't hear it,' she said, dubious once again.

'Do you want me to carry it over to the phone?'

'Don't be silly. Decide what you want, what you think best,' said Ruth, interrupting our conversation.

I realize that to talk about telephones and cars when faced with the great event I was witnessing, is ridiculous. Nothing exists, not a look, not a gesture, not a word, not an object, in the face of the greatness and importance of life and death.

I returned to the kitten and found it had turned on to its other side. It had moved. It had found the strength to move. Perhaps it would recover, perhaps it would heal; slowly, laboriously life might return to it. Not the life of pain, with its stubborn attachment to the world, the life that brings suffering to every living thing that is subject to its laws, but a life triumphant, agile, free of pain. I cried with joy, raising my fists to the sky. 'You're going to win! You're going to win!' I yelled. I decided to devote all my strength to healing the little patient. I brought it, wrapped in the rag, close to my bed, gave it a little more milk and went to sleep.

My brother appeared to me in a dream: he was smiling at me trustingly, a bright light surrounded his face, but when he turned around I saw that his neck had been crushed. I shouted with horror and woke up. It was a sunny morning, as though nothing had happened in the universe.

I leaned out of bed, to see if the kitten was still alive. I hoped it was with all my heart, with all my capacity for hope. The rag I had wrapped it in was soaked with blood and excrement, like the seat of my Volvo, but there was no sign of the little creature. I peered around, looking for traces of blood, I knelt down to look under the bed. The kitten had disappeared, as though sucked into a void.

'Where are you?' I murmured. Then a growing and

inexplicable fury seized hold of me. A thousand times I rebuked myself for my stupid act of pity, which I now considered false. I feared that this little being, condemned to death, had sullied, infected the whole house kept so scrupulously tidy by myself and the old cleaning lady who had looked after me for almost twenty years. I was already imagining having to call in a fumigating company after the kitten's death, but in the meantime I wondered where it had disappeared to, how it had managed to drag itself to wherever it was now. I looked everywhere, even taking out my cupboard drawers. Nothing. The kitten wasn't there. I didn't know whether to leave the house, who knew what spectacle I would find upon my return. I was a prisoner of my rash rebellion against the presence of death on life's horizon.

But now what was I to do? If that damned creature was dead in some hidden corner of my house, only the stench of its decomposition would reveal its hiding place.

Why had it fled? Why had it refused my attentions, the milk, the warmth? Was everything pointless? Did it mean that nothing existed but victims and murderers? Emotion, pity, tenderness, were they mere illusion? Was everything governed solely by the base, dark law of nature?

I quickly got dressed, picked up my old leather brief-case and set off for the office. Throughout my car journey I was tormented by the idea that beneath the newspapers on the back seat there was the blood and excrement of the wounded kitten, which was by now certainly dead under a cushion in some corner of my lovely house. It would be found by the cleaning lady who, that very day, would be coming down from her attic by the public wash-houses to do my cleaning.

Once I reached the office all the fear and dismay passed. Suddenly I was deluged in files, business, contracts. Ruth rang me at midday.

'I'm coming over. Yes, I'm going to come and get you. I'm taking the train at three. I'll be with you at seven.'

'What about your patients?' I asked.

'I don't know which is stronger, my love for you or my pity for them. At the moment I know I have to help you. I feel you're disturbed. Your brother . . .'

'Yes. I can't find peace. I can't accept his fate.'

'I'll be with you at seven,' said Ruth, abruptly terminating the conversation.

A moment later, keen and desperate, the kitten's voice echoed around my office.

'I've understood now. It was all just a dream,' I murmured, since that fatally wounded, paralysed animal could not have followed me to my office.

'Or maybe it's a different cat that just happens to be here by coincidence,' I thought. 'Obsession produces coincidences like that.'

I scanned the office, which was both well appointed and untidy. There was no sign of a cat. I pinched myself to check that I was awake.

'Pinching yourself, how ridiculous,' I thought. Once more the frail, desperate and heart-rending cry of the kitten rang out. I listened hard, and at the third cry I worked out which direction it was coming from. With a leap I reached my leather briefcase resting on a table, and noticed that it was open. The day before I had left it by the radiator, a couple of feet from the improvised bed of the dying animal. I pushed aside the strap. Yes, the kitten was there, at the bottom. Perhaps, in its agony, it had been desperately trying to escape everyone's gaze. Perhaps with one final effort it had hoped to find a safe place where it could take refuge, no longer persecuted and tormented by its murderer.

'Oh my God, my papers!' I exclaimed the moment I saw the little creature at the bottom of the bag. Very important contracts, official letters and documents were drenched with blood, saliva and vomit. All the work I had done over the previous two months was now obliterated, unusable! And yet that was not my first thought. 'It's still alive!' my conscience told me. 'It can still be comforted, it can still be stroked, before death consumes it.' That was my first thought. A minute later I called my secretary.

'Bring me a glass of warm milk, please,' I said. My secretary looked at me in surprise.

'And a boiled egg?' she asked. 'Toast?'

'I'm not going to have breakfast today, thanks,' I stammered. My secretary walked out, dumbfounded.

She probably thought I was ill. She came back two minutes later with a glass of warm milk. But there was no spoon.

'Please go back to the bar and bring me a spoon.'

'A . . .'

'Yes. I need one. How can you drink milk without a spoon?'

'Why?' asked my secretary. I didn't give her an explanation.

'Go on!' I shouted. The moment the door closed the kitten started miaowing.

'It could give me away,' I thought. 'The dying beast could reveal itself in front of everyone, a shameful mark of myself.' Death and horror would be the mark by which everyone would know me. I didn't know what to do. Perhaps I myself should . . . No! Not kill it! Never. Become its murderer . . . Never.

I shut my briefcase in the iron cupboard and waited for my secretary to come back. In the meantime I took a few sips of milk. 'That way she'll think it's for me,' I thought.

When my secretary came back with the teaspoon I acted as though nothing was wrong and dismissed her, looking irritated and absorbed. Then I took the briefcase out of the cupboard and, taking every precaution, wrapping it in a handkerchief, I took the kitten out of the bloody tangle of the papers.

It was breathing laboriously, painfully. I forgot everything: the office, the house, my love of Ruth, life. I thought only of giving a moment of comfort to that poor damned animal: to my brother, to myself.

I put it down on the table, picked up the glass of milk and tried to pour it into its mouth. It opened its mouth, but only to emit a long and feeble lament. I tried and tried again, without success.

'What's wrong with you? Don't you want to go on living?' I asked. The reply that reached my ears was sudden and terrifying. The little beast clumsily pulled itself up, attempted a few rickety steps, tumbled from the table and went on dragging itself around the office, leaving traces of blood and bile everywhere.

'I'm ruined,' I thought. The only thing that occurred to me was to call my secretary. I threw open the door and shouted, 'Come here! Come here immediately!'

My secretary ran in and the minute she saw the scene she erupted into strident, unbridled shrieks.

'Help! Help! A monster! Help!'

After a few seconds, two or three ushers appeared in the doorway, then some employees arrived, mostly young, and they all contemplated the sort of arena my office had been turned into. There were traces of filth on the carpet, stains of blood on the furniture. A young employee took a step forward.

'You've got to kill that vermin!' he stammered, lifting his foot to crush the kitten that was dragging itself slowly around in a circle.

'No! Don't you dare kill it, or . . .'

The boy looked at me in terror. He took a step back.

'He's gone mad,' he murmured and left the office, pushing his way through the small crowd.

I picked the kitten off the ground, wrapped it in some white sheets of paper that I kept on my desk for my appointments.

'You can't understand . . . pity . . . the soul . . . a living creature . . . life . . .'

They all stood there astonished, like so many gods, judges of life and death.

My fate was settled. I had lost all the prestige I had earned myself through years of work. These people moved aside and let me past, or rather they threw me out – that was how it felt – like a leper.

I took a taxi. 'Take me to the nearest animal hospital,' I said to the taxi driver.

'What?' he exclaimed. I repeated the request.

'I don't know of one.'

'Ask head office,' I insisted. The driver obeyed.

Ten minutes later I found myself in front of a shop in whose window snakes coiled and squirrels somersaulted, and there was also a cage full of cocks and hens.

'This is the animal hospital,' the taxi driver said with a smile. 'Good luck, it might get better,' he added nodding towards the kitten.

I went into the shop and told as best I could the story of the little dying animal. The vet, a man of about thirty, tall and blond and wearing gold spectacles, looked at it.

'It's only got a few hours left. Or a few minutes. Perhaps a day. It isn't even worth spending the money for the injection to kill it. Leave it here, if you like.' The kitten twice emitted a weak, graceful, disarming miaow. There was something harmonious in the little voice, something like a barely audible music, a song.

'Thank you,' I said. I turned around and left, with the kitten in my arms. I went back towards the office, like a thief, hugging the walls so as not to be seen. Then I got into my car and went home. From one day to the next my life had changed completely. There was no turning back, things seemed to be beyond repair.

Opening the door I immediately became aware of Ruth's perfume and a moment later I saw her in front of me, smiling, tender, her arms opened wide, ready to welcome me inside her, as she had done for years. She had taken the first train and arrived earlier than expected. I put the kitten down near the radiator and allowed Ruth's arms to envelop me. We collapsed to the floor, wrapped around one another, and in a moment her sweet breath, her sweet body made me forget all my suffering, all my troubles, the struggle, the pain. 'Life's so generous to me!' I thought. 'It gives me all this joy, this tenderness!' I hugged Ruth even more tightly and quickly prepared to immerse myself in her tender womanhood. The moment she pressed me in her arms I felt something hot on her cheeks: I thought she was weeping with emotion, looked at her and saw to my horror that her face was smeared with blood.

'Your face is all bloody!' I yelled shrilly.

'So is yours! What's happened? What's all this blood?' Ruth said in a stifled voice. I leapt to my feet. I looked at myself in the mirror. Yes, I was covered with blood, as she was, the blood of that filthy creature that was repeating its annoying, irresistible call for help to someone, something that had made it live. It was laying claim to life. It was near to us, on the carpet that the cleaning lady had just cleaned.

We washed ourselves.

'I've come for half an hour. I can't stay. I'm sorry. Please, don't torment yourself, be yourself again.'

'I've always been myself. Too much so,' I said. I was beaten. We got dressed in silence. Ruth, like the gentle stranger from the Bible, said goodbye, stroking the back of my neck and repeating, clear-eyed: 'Don't torment yourself. Come with me, we can be together tonight if you like.'

'And that poor creature?'

'It'll die. It'll die in peace.'

'Look how it's dragging itself about, how it's shaking. I'm going to try and give it something to eat. I think there's still plenty of life, plenty of life in it,' I said.

'I've got to go. Forgive me,' Ruth whispered, almost weeping. 'You can join me, if you like.'

She left. I remained alone with the cat, which began miaowing quietly, desperately. I understood that I had to choose, at least as long as the animal remained alive, between it and my love, between a fatally wounded animal and a tender human being, filled with love, alive and thoughtful. 'What choices!' I exclaimed internally. 'What choices we have to make!'

All of a sudden I remembered Dr Schmidt. 'Perhaps he can help me,' I thought. 'This cat has dwelt within me for who knows how long, and now its ghost is assuming material form. Maybe by going backwards I'll discover where it begins, where the figure of the dying animal makes its first appearance in my imagination, in my soul.'

I called Dr Schmidt and, laughing, sobbing, I told him the story of those two days.

'Please, help me. Come here, if you can,' I begged.

'I can't, I'm sorry,' murmured Dr Schmidt. 'Maybe tomorrow.'

'But I need you now. It's now that I'm tormenting myself in this stupid way. If only you could see what it's like! Not the pity of the waking mind, but something more profound. I don't even know myself.' Then Dr Schmidt introduced the argument of the endlessness of the natural world. Imagine a doctor talking about things like that!

'Calm down. Think of your love. Of something beautiful. Think of the Himalayas lit by the sun, deserted, inviolate, eternal. Think of the absence and the presence of your lady, and of Him who presides over the laws of the universe. Think of something infinite.' That's what Dr Schmidt said to me that time.

'The Himalayas are exactly what I'm thinking about as I look at this alien, unexpected guest, this wounded, desperate creature. The infinite is here and there and we are at the point where everything meets, life and death, ignorance and knowledge, madness and wisdom, love and lovelessness, goodness and evil, victim and murderer. We are here, immobilized, transfixed, beaten,' I shouted. I begged his help. But he, as perhaps befits a doctor, wouldn't be dragged into this whirlpool of emotions.

'Calm down,' said Schmidt. 'Everything will sort itself out. That's what always happens. Nature sorts everything out.'

'Nature! Where everything eats everything else!'

'Goodnight. Get some rest. Tomorrow it'll be over,' said the doctor, not wanting to listen to my laments any more. Is it right for a doctor to show such detachment towards his patient, or should he allow himself to be involved in an emotional, human relationship? Is it right that someone who presides over everything should treat us with such indifference?

I shall finish my story. The next day the kitten was still not dead. It was miaowing in a really terrible, harrowing way. At that point I decided. I wrapped it in a white rag – the cat was grey, neutral – went down the stairs and put it near the rubbish bin. 'That's what they do with us, too. We end up among the garbage, the offal,' I thought. I stayed and watched for a while. No one came, no one went into the house. I realized that at the end of the day

I was even more ruthless than the young workman who would have killed the kitten, stamping it to death, if I hadn't stood in his way.

I took the train and went to see Ruth. But my love was poisoned. The image of the wounded animal wouldn't let me be. 'Victim and murderer, that's our fate. Cain and Abel. Or perhaps both at the same time. How difficult it is!' I thought. The train. The best idea I had was to take the train and go . . . go . . . wander, as man wanders through life. And this is the end of my story.

I could have produced so much, become rich and famous, and instead . . . for ten years I have been living in inertia, passively, like a beggar. A final thing.

If my story seems too bitter, to comfort you, since I have obliged you to read these lines, I could say that I stayed with the kitten, that I healed it, and that I have shared a love with Ruth that was happy, tender, free of shadows. But I fear that such a lie would be even more tragic, since man's capacity to bear the pain of existence, and indeed to draw inspiration from it, and thus a reason for joy, is the true marvel of creation.

Respectfully yours,

S. G.

MESSAGE FOR THE CENTURY

In memory of Gustavo Fischer, lawyer

1

The extraordinary things that have happened to me in my life, my ideas that have become irreversible deeds, will be narrated in the words that follow. I am not talking about books, pages, chapters: by the time my story reaches you, books made of paper may no longer exist, and even words will be replaced by ideograms like those in the Chinese language. I cannot imagine with any exactitude the form in which this story will finally arrive with you. In order to communicate it I shall use all the means now at man's disposal. This is one of them. Perhaps my story will not reach anyone, and its reality will be swallowed by the void. But if anyone receives this message, I should like to ask him to imagine the person who sent it: a man who lived in the final decades of the period of time that is conventionally, in the western countries, called the twentieth century.

This man lives at the centre of a villa, a two-storey building of bedrooms and vast halls. I would like everyone to see me, at least in their mind's eye, sitting in my wheelchair, as I roll around the rooms, my body stiff, with very short arms and legs and a torso swollen with fat, because, seized with the anguish of being born deformed, all I have done is eat. Forgive me if I invade your mind with these images: as you shall see, in a sense you can draw consolation from them rather than worrying unnecessarily. The shape of my head, in any case, is perfectly normal, even if its movements are uncontrollable. Sometimes my eyes roll back, my jaw contracts and relaxes, drawing grimaces of pain and tension on my face. My double chin constantly swells and subsides like the wattles of a turkey. My short, twisted legs grow agitated, my arms grope randomly through the air. I have lived like this for thirty-five years. I was born like this. Why?

It was not due to a hereditary defect. I came into the world affected by these disabilities because my mother, a desperately vain woman, unable to expel me from her belly and rather than have herself cut open, demanded that I be pulled out with a kind of pincer used by doctors, called a forceps. This instrument, crushing my head, severed some of my nerve centres. A servant confided all of this to me shortly before my mother's death.

But my father, too, had a cruel part to play in this story. Some of his decisions, taken when I was still a child, had as much influence on me as those of my mother.

These two people were the instruments with which life sought to punish me. Until now I have resisted the pain. I am not a compliant monster. I am capable of making great efforts, of conceiving great ideas and feeling great emotions.

I was still in the cradle when I realized that my body resisted any act of will. If I wanted to grasp an object that was held out to me, off went that extremity known as my hand, in a different direction to the one my will intended. Touched by the rays of the sun that came in through the window, I wanted to stay still and enjoy the warmth, like that of the maternal womb which I had recently left. I couldn't do so. My muscles were shot through by meaningless stimuli and my limbs stretched and stirred, my head twisted on my neck. I was a living question, even before I knew what a question was. There was no cause behind those lightning flashes that struck me. What's this? my being shrieked, and received no reply. I was a sort of electric chair to myself. When my mother repeated certain words to me for hour upon hour, trying to teach me to pronounce them, I heard a horrible bleating noise coming from my mouth, absolutely unlike the pleasant acoustic phenomenon that was her gentle voice. And yet I tried to repeat those sounds, which I soon came to associate with the face that first appeared before me. It was thus that I learned to pronounce the word 'mama'.

It takes me an enormous effort to pronounce words one after another. The muscles of my tongue and my mouth oppose any regular operation, so I must often break down my speech syllable by syllable. On other occasions, making an extreme effort, I am forced to talk too quickly, and hurtle headlong towards the end of my sentences.

I know everything about my childhood. With the help of a doctor I have recovered the memory of my life as a newborn. Through the medium of hypnosis, this young doctor is able to make his patients' minds regress to the foetal state and beyond: to a former life. One day I read an account of his work in a journal with the curious name of *Rhizome*. My secretary eventually found the doctor's address, contacted him, fixed a date for the meeting, which occurred here, in my villa. Our long sessions began . . . The normal techniques of hypnosis had no effect on me: the little keyring moving back and forth before my eyes, the calm voice of the doctor trying to persuade me to close my eyelids, 'heavy, growing heavier and heavier' gave me muscular contractions. I began to move my limbs, to cough, to twist my neck. They had to give me a tranquillizer.

After many attempts, Dr F. came up with a strategy. One day he turned up at my house with a tape-recorder. A deafening noise issued from two portable speakers. At first my reactions to this stimulus were terrible: my arms made sudden movements, my legs began to shake, my whole body jerked. But after a minute of this crazy dance, the rumble overcame the strength of my muscular stimuli, and my organism calmed down. After ten minutes I fell into a state of hypnosis. Rock music has this effect on me: it agitates me and calms me down at the same time.

On another machine, as we have established, Dr F. recorded the entire conversation that passed between us during that first session. It was thus that I was able to hear my own voice, the bleating, the wheezing, and the calm, honest questions of the doctor. The conversation revolved around old and innocent memories: the truth about the first years of my life had not yet emerged.

I see myself in the cradle, I feel certain mysterious, enormous levers (someone's hands and arms) lifting me into the air, causing me to have terrifying muscular contractions. I feel something huge and warm coming towards my mouth, a sweet and tepid liquid descending into me: the breast of the mother nursing me. On my body I feel the contact of something warm and smooth, my mother's hand. Everything moves at a terrible speed before my eyes, which gradually distinguish all the things moving jerkily about: the world around us. I spend a long time in that continuous chaos, in that unstoppable movement, and I feel a searing pain, then I begin to distinguish those sounds that are repeated with irritating obstinacy. Every now and again a big, formless voice beats down upon me – my father's voice – and a clear, harmonious voice caresses and envelops me – my mother's. In my brain, gripped by panic, language begins to take shape.

There is also a third shape, mobile and sonorous, which appears from time to time. It is my nurse. Her hands grip my legs and pull them in an attempt to make them accomplish slow and regular movements. These operations plunge me into an unbearable state of tension. My muscles stiffen, becoming a huge, hard mass, a stupid puppet nailed to itself, awkward and heavy.

These three faces were the first to appear to me. Sometimes I also saw a fourth face which gave off a strange and bitter smell: it was my doctor, Dr Spitzer, a paediatrician. At first his glasses frightened me, those terrible great circles gleamed menacingly, all the more so since two other dark and glowing circles moved within them: his eyes. That face didn't stretch as obstinately the other three, it didn't pull my legs and hands, all it did was touch me. The sound that came from that soft thing (its mouth) was light and low, it didn't frighten me. 'Stay like that for ever,' it said on one occasion. For two or three years I tried to solve the puzzle of those words, until one day I understood. Then I began to hate even the doctor who had treated me during the first years of my life, to spit and defecate in his face.

Every new word I learned was preceded by hate and terror. Usually the first time I shouted it with rage, I yelled it at the top of my voice, as if with contempt. Some of Dr F.'s recordings faithfully reconstruct those stages of my mental and physical development. I can assert in all honesty that I am not exaggerating in my description. I find the experiment of hypnosis miraculous: I could never have supposed that the voice of an adult could return to the sounds emitted by a newborn. Anyone still sceptical about this assertion can put it to the test with the help of a good medical hypnotist.

Recently, during my stormy love affair with Dora, I tried to cancel out the terrible impressions of my first years of life, and perhaps sometimes I even succeeded. But more of that later.

Is it possible that within me language is not associated with some more positive sentiment such as gratitude, carnal pleasure, affection? I don't know. The only thing I can claim with any certainty is the unimaginable pain I endured in appropriating the correct use of language.

During those years there was a young poet living in town who, in open defiance of civil society, taught his son, the same age as myself, not to talk but to bark. The poet died of hunger at the age of twenty-two. The last months of his life he had spent in a cage. His wife and son survived him. His widow, at a distance of more than thirty years, is working on the first complete edition of the works of that rebellious spirit. I would have been grateful to my parents if they had spared me the trouble of ordering my lips, my lungs, my tongue, if they had not forced me to emit those sounds that they never tired of repeating to me. I would have preferred to bark as well, to express only rage and contentment: that was forbidden to me. They wanted to teach me all the tricks of language.

The poison of the word entered me, never to leave the cells of my body.

But there was something worse in the constriction of the word. In their obstinacy, my parents took it into their heads to make me overcome the physical obstacles of my nature. First in turn, then both together, they began to hold me by the hand. With my arms stretched up, my hands in theirs, I was forced with blows from my parents' knees to advance towards some stable destination: a table, a chair, the lavatory. If I stopped or hesitated, or if I was paralysed by the contractions of my muscles, a blow to the spine forced me to move. 'Why should I move?' I asked myself. 'Where should I go? Why there and not here? Will I feel better after I've made this dreadful effort?' I didn't understand the meaning of those forced actions, of that absurd movement from one place to the next. All the more so in that my muscles wouldn't go along with me. But the worst was still to come. Mama and Papa had decided to turn me into a man like other men, and they were willing to make any sacrifice just to achieve their purpose.

They had some Swedish wall-bars fixed to the wall, rungs of rounded wood, given a light varnish and lacquered. In theory, by clutching on to these bars, I would eventually be able to climb to the ceiling, but that was just the theory. The parallel bars were installed along all the internal walls of the house, so as to allow me to walk all around the villa. I never tried to do it.

After several afternoons spent trying to climb the wall-bars, I had an epiphany. I climbed a few bars (it took me half an hour) and suddenly let go and fell to the floor. I felt an indescribable pain, heard the shrieks of the nurse, the terrified cries of my mother, and finally my father's rough, low voice. Other people I had never seen before also came running. They carefully picked me up: the fracture of several bones caused me excruciating pain.

They carried me into my room and laid me out on the little bed. I was screaming at the top of my voice, weeping and cursing.

There was a great hubbub around me, noisier than anything I could manage myself. They carried me out, down the stairs, into the deafening, dusty street, to Papa's car. I was breathless from shouting, from the effort to confront my pain and hatred. I was transferred to a revolting place whose smell immediately made me throw up. It was a hospital. They put me in a cot again, a man with great black hairs over his lip touched me, and a moment later I sank into the dark void.

'Well, Abramo!' shouted the face with its great dark hairs. At that shout I woke up. I answered with the only sentence I knew how to pronounce correctly at the time.

'Here I am,' I said. It was a phrase I had once heard from my father, and which I imitated to perfection, with my little voice like the yapping of a small dog. Dr F. led me back to this event a number of times. That was how I came to understand that the phrase 'here I am' was also the feeble sign with which I wanted to signal my existence, and my uncontainable rage at being exposed to the world's vexations.

It was months before I could go back home. Not that I didn't like being in the Salus Clinic where I had recovered. Indeed, the constant attentions of the nurses and doctors gratified me much more than the caresses of my nurse. Mama and Papa came to see me every day, smiling at me and demonstrating all their affection. I could no longer deal with that affection, which caused me such painful and useless exertions.

The day came for me to go back home. In my very best clothes, I was picked up into my father's arms. A few minutes later I found myself surrounded once more by the hateful wall-bars, the majolica, the paintings, the precious vases, all the junk with which my parents expressed their taste.

The day after my release from the clinic my mother wanted to start painting my portrait. The sun was very bright that morning, my mother's studio, with its broad windows, was filled with blinding light. My mother made me wear a peaked hat, sat me up in an armchair facing her easel and started to look at me, to turn me around, to stroke me, to look at me again.

'You're handsome,' she said, starting to cry. She wept desperately, I remember how her shoulders shook, how the smooth skin of her face was bathed in tears. 'You're as beautiful as the sun,' she repeated. I couldn't understand what was happening and, just feeling admiration for her, for her beauty, I opened my mouth, and after many attempts I managed to emit a sound, a little grunt, the same obscene word that I had heard the chauffeur saying so many times, and which I myself shouted at moments of the greatest desperation.

I was attracted by my mother and yet I said that word to her. She raised her eyes to me. I remember the strangeness of her expression. She started to cry and sob even more loudly, even more desperately, and I repeated the word again. My mother leaped to her feet, came towards me with the fury of a wild beast, and started to beat my face, my hands, my legs.

'Shut up!' she shrieked, and I began to cry with all my strength, until I had run out of breath, and to shout my outrage at her. After giving me such a terrible beating, Mama came to her senses and began to stroke me, to press me to her breast, to kiss my hair, my neck, my hands, groaning like someone wounded. 'Forgive me, I beg you, forgive me! Nothing has happened, nothing, nothing.'

She picked me up, carried me to the bathroom, washed my bloody face and my hands, changed my little suit, my vest, and went on petting me as she murmured: 'You're the most beautiful of them all. My love, my lamb, my treasure, I'll never leave you, never, ever, ever.' She sat me in the armchair, facing the easel. I was terrified by her blows, but I was still filled with an awful rage, a sense of outrage that would not be erased. After a while, my brain was filled with a great drowsiness and I fell asleep.

I woke up in my cot. Above me was my mother, her face. All of a sudden I remembered what had happened and, with a great effort, turned my face to the wall so as not to see my mother's face, so beautiful. She gripped me by the head and once again she turned my face towards her. Our eyes surveyed one another. It was a terrible moment. I don't know how, but I understood that I had to concentrate all my strength into my eyes: all other movements would have been as convulsive and uncontrolled as ever. I managed to bring my eyelids and my pupils to a standstill, to stare into my mother's eyes, while my arms and legs moved, jerking around with agitation. With a greater effort of will than I had ever attempted before I transferred all of myself into the fixity of that look; my mother turned away, discomfited. That will, that energy of life, revealed itself to my consciousness.

A few years passed. I won't speak of the violence with which they forced me once again to walk, clutching the wall-bars, to pick up a spoon and a fork between my hands which never managed to hit the target, to learn not only the words of the language in which my mother and father communicated amongst themselves, but also those of two other languages, English and German.

One morning the servant came to clean my room, as she did every day. Suddenly I understood that that morning I would learn the secret of my infirmity and decide the whole of my future. I was nine years old.

'Come here,' I said to the old Romanian maid. She looked at me in surprise. I had never spoken to her, if that is the right word for the painful mooing noise that issued from my mouth.

'Come here!' I shouted. The old lady came over.

'My child,' she murmured, touched.

'What is it?' I asked. My arms and legs began to stir slowly, vaguely, like the feet of an insect.

'What is what?' the old lady replied. She looked at me in fear. Her breathing was laboured.

'This.' I nodded with my chin towards my stiffened limbs.

'My child,' she whispered. Then she leaned over me, with her broom in her hand, and began kissing my cheeks.

'Go away!' I shouted. As I did so, my legs recoiled. The old lady, even more frightened than before, took three steps backwards.

'What do you want from me?' she asked in her bad Italian.

'Why do I do this?' Once again I nodded my chin towards my legs and my arms. 'Why?'

'Ask at school, ask the teacher,' answered the servant, with a certain degree of mean obstinacy.

'They won't tell me anything. You have to tell me.'

'Ask your mother!' the old lady raised her voice. She was really frightened.

'No. My mother doesn't tell me anything. Papa never talks to me. You have to tell me. Now –' At which point I was already exhausted by the exertion of emitting so many sounds, so much breath, and jerking my limbs about.

'I don't know anything,' the old lady groaned, with the handle of her broom under her arm, wringing her hands.

'You have to tell me or I'll kill you,' I managed to say, after an enormous effort. The old woman looked at me first with compassion, then with terror. I had been staring into her eyes. She saw my will becoming an expression. She approached again, slowly; she was going to overcome my will with her caresses, her tenderness, her apparent love.

'Go away!' I said again. She stayed close to me and asked in a low voice, 'What do you want to know?'

'Why am I like this? What is this?'

The old woman began to stammer and jabber words in her language and mine; then she fell silent again.

'Why?' I asked stubbornly. The will of that simple woman, who had seen wars, death, suicides, massacres, revolutions, was broken in the face of mine. At some point the servant made up her mind and, amid great confusion, and with many absurd expressions, the fruit of truth and lies, she told me everything: my mother's desperation, after the nine months of waiting were long since past and she still couldn't give birth to me, or 'give me light' as we say, the atrocious pains that uselessly afflicted her: the placenta in which I was wrapped which still wouldn't break, and how I continued to stay inside her, practically clinging to her guts, not wanting to relinquish the hold that assured me of the food, the oxygen and the water that I needed. My mother cried out for days on end because of those continuous pains, the cramps, the agony diffused throughout her whole body, and I couldn't bring myself to be born. She cursed against fate, against life, against fertility, until my father, tormented by the horrific spectacle, asked the doctor to free her from her suffering by carrying out the operation known as 'Caesarean section'.

'No!' shrieked my mother, and in imitation of her the servant-woman made a broad gesture that represented exaggeration. 'No, please don't cut me, I'm not a bag to be slit open, I'm a human being!'

According to the servant, faced with my mother's desperation, the doctor ordered her to be taken to his clinic immediately where, by means of manual pressure, injections and pills, he would help her to free herself of me, without an operation. She was taken to the clinic (the servant told of the turmoil, the effort required to lift someone so debilitated by the effort of childbirth, my father's anxiety) and, after two days my body began to appear between my mother's legs. But I still didn't want to leave that warm, protective lair. To take me out without cutting my mother's belly, and that was something she opposed with all her might, he resorted to the forceps, which crushed my head, severing some of my nerve centres. At this point in the story the servant hid her face in her hands, then looked at me and said: 'It's your fault that all this happened. Why didn't you want to be born?' Her voice, suddenly secure and firm, her severe and accusatory expression struck me: but the meaning of the question was not entirely comprehensible to me.

'And why did Mama keep me in her belly? Who put me there?' I asked. 'And why wouldn't she have her belly cut to free me?'

'My child!' The old woman murmured, pressing my head to her breast. She smelt of garlic and sweat. Now everything was clear. If I was so unhappy it was down to my mother's decision.

'Thank you,' I said to the servant. 'Don't tell Mama you've told me all about it. And now go.'

The servant took away the bucket of black water and avoided me for a few months. She would go on cleaning our house until her death. When she had passed the age of eighty-six and become completely deaf, she was run over by a bus: she didn't hear the warning horn. She died in hospital, after four months of agony.

As for myself, from the morning of our conversation I began to nurture a desire for revenge. I admired and hated my mother for her beauty and tenderness. I hated and admired my father for his goodness, his love of books, paintings, music. I wanted their faces to vanish from my eye's horizon. Instead they appeared, disappeared, reappeared each day, expressing affectionate concern and cruelty. I didn't feel the slightest gratitude for their efforts. What was there to be grateful for? Being reduced to these conditions? Being made to pay for the fruit of their intercourse, and their insane desire for affection and dominion in the eyes of a child? No. I would be grateful for nothing. All the more since as time passed I discovered certain things about my father, and especially about my mother, which left me shattered. The opportunity for revenge had arrived.

2

I was eleven years old. It was the year I felt and saw a part of my body becoming erect. A part of me, some of whose functions I was unaware of, and which I was to discover one day while the nurse was giving me a bath.

'Look, the mast of the ship!' I tried to say to the nurse, with my clucking voice. Even today I can hear the echo of that exclamation of mine. Yes, there in the middle of my body I suddenly saw a piece of my flesh growing erect. I couldn't understand what it might be. During the intervals between one lesson and another, my schoolmates talked only of how the man puts a part of himself into the woman. But I couldn't understand what part that could be. With the constant agitation of my limbs, I couldn't imagine how such an act could be accomplished. That day the nurse burst out laughing.

'What are you laughing at?' I asked, with a massive effort. I was agitated and couldn't speak in a clear and comprehensible way.

'Because you're a man now,' the nurse said with a contemptuous laugh, giving a little tap to the part of my body that had become erect, just below my belly. I didn't understand.

The next day I talked about it with the boy who sat next to me in class, a blond boy who helped me sit on the bench beside him every morning, and who sometimes switched on the machine with which I had learned to write. (It was a little machine with a ribbon of paper in it. By pressing certain very large buttons I managed to write: it would have been impossible for me to grip and move a pen or a pencil, instruments which were then in use around the world. The letters that formed words and sentences were printed on the ribbon. It took me five months to learn to write. Today I wouldn't bother. Written words don't count any more. Other signs, other images fill our imagination.)

'Try and touch yourself,' my classmate suggested. 'It's brilliant when you do that.' All manner of other things were explained to me that morning, amidst laughter and words whispered in secret. But I couldn't touch myself. My condition precluded that form of pleasure: 'An orang-utan, a chimpanzee can do it, and I can't,' I repeated to myself, when someone explained to me that the privilege of pleasuring oneself was granted only to monkeys and man. 'So I'm less than a monkey!' I thought. I was filled with a terrible rage. All the more so since what had happened in the bath that morning was happening to me more and more often, and more and more often a feeling of terrible tension ran through my whole body, my brain, my belly, and there, in between my legs.

'What is this?' I wondered, baffled and afraid. 'What's happening to me?' My whole body, my being was shaken by that thing that I can now identify as instinct. Instinct! Who planted it in us? Why does it exist? Is its sole purpose to preserve life? Do hunger, thirst, fear, sleep and sex exist solely to transmit life? How can you explain the strength, the terror of those attacks of instinct and my inability to satisfy them? Every time I felt that sensation I felt happy and desperate. I wanted to die. It was during this time that I began to torture my mother. Certain events, certain terrifying discoveries suggested the idea that I could, that I had to do it.

One February morning at around ten o'clock, when I was still in bed, I was once again ambushed by that intoxicating and tormenting sensation. I hadn't gone to school: it had snowed and frozen during the night, and it was impossible to go into town in the car. When I became aware of that sudden dark and snarling force within me I started shouting as loud as I could, in my nasal, clucking voice. 'Mama!' The word echoed around the whole house, or rather 'Memmee! Memmee!', since I had never

been able to master the clear pronunciation of the letter
'a'. I yelled for ten minutes until I heard footsteps coming
up the wooden stairs. A moment before my mother
opened the door I pulled back the covers and stayed there,
naked. My mother came in without losing her compo-
sure. 'Cover yourself up, my child, or you'll catch a cold,'
she said, like a professional. What? My nudity, my erec-
tion meant nothing to her? I tried to arrange myself in
such a way the better to show her that strange, temporary
protuberance that marked my excitement. 'Gently, gently.
Let's cover ourselves up. What can you be thinking
about?'

My mother's indifference irritated me.

'Take it,' I bleated, breathlessly.

'What did you say?'

'Take it! Like you do with the gardener. I've seen you,
you know.'

She grabbed me by the shoulders and shook me three
or four times.

'Beast,' she shrieked.

'You're the beast! Filthy slut!' I shouted. My mother
gave me a terrific slap, then another and yet another.

'You're a pig! You've made me this way just so as not to
mess up your damned belly. So you can give your belly to
the gardener.'

My mother went on hitting me, then threw herself on
the floor and started crying, howling. 'I'm going to kill
myself! I'm going to kill myself!'

'Why are you telling me? What do you think I care if you kill yourself? Go ahead and do it.'

'You're a monster,' she cried. She regretted it immediately, but the poisoned arrow was already burning within me.

'You've made me like this, you ugly whore. Off you go and kill yourself. Go on.' I was offended to the very depths of my being, I never wanted to see that stupid, vulgar woman again. 'Off you go and kill yourself, I tell you! Off you go! Or go to your gardener and have him give you a good old grope!'

My mother ran off. I waited with my heart in my mouth for the sign, any sign of her death. No one came to tell me anything. When they brought me down to dinner, she turned up as well. She acted as though nothing had happened, she was as majestic, ethereal and smiling as ever: a kind of artfully created image.

'Good evening, Mama,' I greeted her, looking at her with a stupid expression.

'Good evening, my child,' she answered, with a smile of polite superiority.

'Are you back from seeing the gardener?' I asked, looking at Papa, then at her, then at the old servant-woman. My mother blushed. Her translucent face was flushed with blood.

'Are you back from seeing the gardener? I see you with him every evening while Papa's in his study. He works and you pretend to paint in the greenhouse, when really you're getting your clothes off and writhing with the gardener.'

It was Papa's turn. He was a mild-mannered man, from another country, and therefore always a little circumspect, but at that moment he became furious: he leaped to his feet and began to beat me with all his strength. He slapped and punched me, and I couldn't defend myself or weep because I was completely breathless.

'Leave him alone!' my mother shrieked. 'Leave him alone!' But Papa went on for a few moments, and then she ran away, yelping like a dog. Papa stopped hitting me.

'Is what you said true? Did you see it?' he asked, panting.

'Yes, yes, yes!' I bleated.

'Swear you saw it!'

'Is it because I'm like this that you won't believe me?'

Papa looked thunderstruck. He threw himself into an armchair. He began to sob.

A few minutes later a horrendous scream echoed down the corridor. The Romanian servant-woman came running. 'Quick, sir! Run! Madam is . . .'

My father shook himself. I was there crammed into a corner and unable to breathe, everything around me looked purple.

I never saw Mama alive again. The house was deserted. My father came back late in the evening, he didn't even come to say hello to me. I heard him talking to the servant-woman, then he spent all night walking up and

down above my head, in his private study. It was the servant who told me what had happened.

'Rat poison. Madam injected herself with rat poison.
She's vomiting blood, she's blind. She's going to die,' the
gaunt old woman reported to me in the morning four
days later, bringing me my coffee and feeding it to me
with abrupt twists of the hand, as though she wanted to
asphyxiate me with the spoon.

The image of my mother appeared before my eyes
again, projected itself onto my brain cells. I saw her again,
white, blonde and agile as she writhed in the arms of the
gardener, until, two days later, Papa came to dress me
and had the chauffeur carry me to the car and then down
the steps to a hospital mortuary where Mama was lying
on a slab, covered by a sheet.

My father uncovered her face. 'Look at her!' he whispered.

'No!' I whispered back. 'I don't want to see her.'

'Look at her! Look what you've reduced her to!'

'Look what she's reduced me to.'

'You're not leaving here until you've seen her,' said my
father and stayed there, waiting. 'You're the way you are,
but you're alive. She's dead.'

'Show her to Paolo,' I murmured. Paolo was the gardener's name.

My father said nothing. Then I opened my eyes and
looked at my mother. I nearly suffocated with horror.
My mother was unrecognizable. Her face was covered

with enormous haematomas. She was yellow, all her features were distorted. She looked like a horrible wax doll. My mother, who had been so beautiful! I was filled with enormous compassion, I began to cry. 'Mama,' I whispered, or rather 'Memmee!', because that was the only way my clucking voice could reproduce the sound which is identical in almost all the languages of the world.

I was taken away. A lot of people came to the funeral, I saw the announcements in the papers. 'After a long and painful death she departed her loved ones . . .' Papa wanted to make his friends and acquaintances believe that nonsense. Everyone played along, as they always do.

That night I couldn't sleep. I was tormented by the vision of my mother. I saw her again in the darkness of my room in many different ways, beautiful and ugly. In the end I pressed the bell and called the servant.

'Come here,' I said to her. 'Touch me, I beg you. Touch me there, please do it.'

'Pig!' muttered the old lady.

'Please. I'm frightened of everything. Everything scares me. Everything hurts me. I beg you . . . It's the only way I'll be able to forget . . .'

'What?'

'Everything. Please.'

The old woman listened. She slipped her hand under the covers, unbuttoned my plastic pants and began to touch me.

'My little man, my tiny little man,' she whispered, weeping. The pleasure made me forget the horror of myself and the world, and after that time every day, even two or three times, I asked the servant to do me the favour which was my only way of cancelling out the anguish and pain at being hurled into my 'self'.

3

I realize that my message to posterity is not an edifying one. But I am convinced that in a sense what I am telling you is. And that is why I ask you to go on following the developments of this story. Please do.

As one might guess, I was left alone with my father, the servant and the three members of our staff: a young cook, my chauffeur who was also my nurse, a manservant. The gardener was fired and for years my father allowed the garden to be invaded by brushwood, by rats and the neighbours' rubbish. Strangely, his attitude towards me changed. He began to dedicate himself to me: he bought me clothes, books, all kinds of toys, he took me abroad to see exhibitions by major artists. We went to Paris, London, Venice two or three times a years. If he could not correct my body, if he could not make it normal, he at least wanted my mind to be out of the ordinary. He bought paintings, statuettes, antique musical instruments. At first, every time he brought home works of art, I was seized by an uncontrollable destructive fury. But I was absolutely incapable of damaging anything. How could I have got close to those paintings, those vases, to break them, if I couldn't even move around on my own? So one evening, while my father – a famous business lawyer but a man of refined culture – was reading me a fragment of Goethe's *Faust*, I interrupted him and bleated my request.

'I want a wheelchair.'

'What? My son condemned to a wheelchair? You've got Eugenio who'll carry you wherever you want.' (Eugenio was the name of the chauffeur at my exclusive service. More than a chauffeur, he was a porter. I was starting to put on weight by now.)

'I don't want to be just a lump. I don't want to depend on the will of a chauffeur.'

'You're free to express any will of your own, through him. He owes you absolute obedience.'

All of a sudden I felt powerful, unstoppable. But I still had one doubt. 'What if I asked him to do something against you?'

'Against me? For what reason?'

'Because you're a damned bourgeois and I'm a super-man!' I said with a laugh. My laughter was like the braying of a donkey, a kind of prolonged sob. My father remained silent.

At this time, I shared my desk at school with a boy of sixteen. He had been held back for three years running. He knew plenty about all kinds of things, about women, priests and life in general. He had read certain books that made him aggressive and contemptuous. He didn't acknowledge any form of solidarity, he left me to wheeze on the bench without lifting a finger, when concentration left me over-excited. He preached virility as a supreme value, and in its name he masturbated during physics lessons, when we were taught by a young supply teacher with inviting breasts.

'You must despise your father, you must kill him, it's the only way you'll be able to free yourself of the curse of your inferior, wicked race,' he said to me one day. He incited me to violence, to the sacrifice of life, to action, I who was unable to do anything against anyone, not even against myself . . . One day he invited me to a demonstration, in a big square in my city. 'How will I get there?' I asked tearfully. Even my weeping was like the braying of a donkey.

'What do I care! Come any way you can. Wriggle like a worm.'

The huge square was full of people of all kinds: toothless, stinking ragamuffins, short-haired middle-class boys, middle-aged men who had just come out of their offices, businessmen rattling with gold. They were all shouting at the tops of their voices, and singing old marches and hymns. In the arms of my chauffeur, who was drenched in sweat, I too tried to shout and sing (my voice was already that of an adult) but, as you may imagine, the effect was grotesque and excruciating. So much so that my friend hurled insults at me and then moved away from me, like someone with the plague. We were carried along by the crowd.

Terrible fights broke out with individuals bearing red neckerchiefs: I saw knives flashing, sticks swinging, chains, knuckle-dusters. Then a cloud of dark smoke filled the square. My driver found it hard to breathe. 'I'm putting you down, I'm leaving you here!' he started to say, and I threatened him: 'I'll get my friends to kill you! Walk, you bastard!' I went on singing and shouting insults against the inferior race, against the traitors to the country, while my legs and arms jerked around at every shot, every shout. I didn't stop until the smoke seemed as though it was going to suffocate me too. Panicking, I yelled at the chauffeur, 'Come on! Come on! Take me home.' Then I fainted.

I woke up in my bed. My father was looking at me sadly. Seeing him like that made me angry.

'Call the chauffeur!' I ordered him. He rang a bell and the butler came, followed by the chauffeur.

'Slap him!' I said.

'Who?' asked the chauffeur, a thin and frightened forty-year-old.

'My father.'

The chauffeur stood there for a moment, then left the room and resigned the same day. After that my father set about buying me a made-to-measure wheelchair with electric commands and sophisticated engineering. He wanted me to excel in that at least. Now I could move as

I saw fit, I was freed from the slavery that nature had imposed on me. First I aimed my wheelchair at a big Chinese vase that had stood in the corridor for years: I struck it head-on, and its fragments nearly blinded me, but I had now accomplished another act of revenge. The glass was removed from all the doors: our house began to assume the look of a bunker.

One morning, after a night of unsettled dreams, I opened my eyes, I looked at the ceiling as usual, trying to find the painting of the mule and the sheep. I heard a noise, looked around and saw my father sitting by my bed with a book in his hands. I saw his lips moving. I looked at the book. It had an ivory cover. It was an old prayer-book. Suddenly I felt as though I've been hurled into a vast space, I was short of breath, I grew pale, I turned purple. My father, a cultivated, cheerful man, in love with beautiful things and beautiful women as my mother had been, had spoken to me a number of times of what lay above us, beneath us, within the invisible earth, within the invisible sky, and each time I had noticed the same dismay in myself as I did that morning. I tried to imagine the world without me! I was terrorized by the very idea. Crippled as I was, I wanted to last for ever. I had seen my mother dead, but I couldn't imagine my own death. Who did my father turn to? Did that thing that filled everything, the eternal, the omnipresent, the ineffable and indescribable really exist? That which speaks up for good in the minds of men?

I couldn't imagine it.

'Put it away!' I said to my father. He closed his book and looked at me for a long time.

'Do you mean it, or are you acting out a part?' I asked. He looked at me.

'You're right. I'm acting a part. I hope it won't be like this for you.' He got to his feet and I didn't see him for two days.

In fact it wasn't like that for me. In my imagination I couldn't see beyond the things that everyone called 'real'. But neither could I conceive of the world without a beginning. Before that beginning, what was there? Who had allowed it to be like that? Chance, that bloodsucker that attaches itself to us? Or a will? In my doubt I refused to reflect in any way. But I didn't act out a part. When the following episode occurred I was eighteen.

One night I was woken by an unusual sound. Dragging footsteps were coming up the stairs. I thought they were those of the old servant, but in fact . . . A few seconds later the door opened and the light came on. I gave an abrupt start with my arms and legs and started howling with fear. My father was there, in the doorway, in his dressing-gown, clutching a sheet of paper, his hair ruffled and his face drenched with tears.

'What do you want? Why won't you leave me in peace?' I bleated.

'Look, I've written my will. I'm taking it to the lawyer

tomorrow. Look how many things I'm leaving you to protect you, to provide for your support for a hundred years. I hope you live that long. I can't go on,' he said, his voice muffled with despair.

'And you're waking me up to tell me that?' I bellowed. 'Go away. Let me sleep. Sleep's the best thing as far as I'm concerned.'

'I know, my son. But I haven't been able to for years. Since you were born.'

'I don't give a damn!' I shouted, wheezing with rage and indignation. 'Shame on you! Shame on you for everything!'

'I feel guilty, as you know, for everything that's happened in this house. I feel guilty.'

'All the more shame on you. Wretch! You're putting your mind at ease with your sense of guilt!' I yelled again. 'Wretch!' I turned over in bed and started grunting and spitting. I wanted to spit in his face but I couldn't. I must confess that today I'm happy I couldn't. Why? Because of what happened a minute later.

My father sat down in a chair, next to the bed, tried to stroke my hair and said to me: 'Guilt is the moving force in the world. Animals don't feel guilt. They don't feel the bite of guilt, just the bite of instinct. Guilt was created, yet it exists, simply, to turn the human being into what he is. Can you understand that?'

'No!' I answered, sobbing, braying like an ass. 'No. No. No.' I was in despair over everything that existed. I would have liked to have erased the world.

'I'm guilty about so many things. And that's why I'm trying to do good for you. All the good I'm capable of. I'm not just leaving you all the money and houses and property, shares, paintings, jewels, gold ingots, I've also opened a bank account for you. You're an adult now. You can do whatever you want with all the money I've put in your account. There's plenty of it. I've been lucky, coming to this country. I want to leave you my whole fortune.'

'What? Your fortune? And mine? Look at me! Look at my fortune! Or are you trying to buy my forgiveness?' I asked with a sob. 'I don't forgive you!'

'I know. But I want to do right by you nonetheless. I can imagine, very vaguely, but I can imagine what you're feeling. And I feel something that isn't just guilt, it's something else. Paternal love. Solidarity. Something an animal would never feel. I might have an accident tomorrow. I'm leaving you with a copy of the will. I'm locking it in this box. Goodbye.' His voice cracked. My father began to weep. He laid his head on the little bedside table and wept. He wept, sobbing quietly. Then he got up, put out the light and went away.

Solidarity. Paternal love. The guilt that moves the world. All his words began to torment my brain. Then, little by little, I started to feel a great sense of contentment. I was rich, I could do whatever I wanted. My mind was suddenly flooded with ideas. The first is easy to guess. The next morning, not having slept a wink all night, I called my father and told him straight out that I wanted to use the first of the money to pay for two or three women. He was obliged to get them for me. I wanted to see a woman naked, just for me. Up until then I'd only seen Mama, in the arms of the gardener. 'Now I want a collection of women, a squad of women, all for me. Other boys my age can flirt with them, choose them, I can't. I can't! You've got to choose them for me.'

'I didn't think you were like that,' said my father. 'Man isn't wicked. Even if he's afflicted in the cruellest way, man isn't necessarily wicked. Now that you've finished school, you could study, cultivate your intelligence, your spirit. I don't want to hear you talking like this.' He left me there, without saying another word.

But that same evening he came back into my room and told me he'd found a woman, a prostitute for me. 'I'll have you brought to her place tomorrow, if you like. But she's not setting foot here.'

'Why not?' I asked, staring at him. Yes, for the third time I expressed my will with my eyes. 'Why not here?'

'This house is . . .' He was going to say 'respectable', I'm sure, but I got in first with such a loud laugh, so like a donkey's bray, so like the noise of a trumpet, so ear-splitting and so long as to leave him completely confused, dazed in the doorway of my room.

'This house is a pigsty! Do you understand me? However much you try and fill it with all your arty hardware, it's a pigsty! Think of Mama. Think of everything that's gone on right here!'

My father's eyes opened wide, dilated like a madman's.

'You're right,' he murmured, then stood there without say anything, convulsively twisting the belt of his very smart suit.

'What are you waiting for? Go and sleep!' I said. And he, a miserable, suffering figure, could do nothing but go down the stairs and disappear into the darkness. At one o'clock in the morning I called the manservant whose duty it was to take me to the lavatory. Before he picked me up as usual to carry me to the bathroom, I whispered to him: 'Go outside and you'll find the usual prostitutes out by the station. Bring the two youngest and prettiest here. I'll pay you nicely for your trouble. Look, here's the stamp for signing the cheques, here's the book. Bring them to me. Do it quietly, so that no one hears. You have to be here in half an hour.' The crook didn't think twice, he set off immediately to satisfy my request. I have seldom enjoyed myself as I did that evening, albeit for entirely unpredictable reasons.

While the servant was out I started to tremble, my teeth chattered with the emotion of being about to make love for the first time. I poured on a whole bottle of aftershave: by gratifying the olfactory sense I hoped to become less repellent in the visual. Finally the servant came back: I heard his cautious steps climbing the stairs, I saw the door slowly opening, and a moment later, in the semi-darkness, I saw two strangely dressed prostitutes, with plastic shopping-bags over their arms, two old mothers, anxious and frightened. The light went on, my limbs moved around like creatures independent of my trunk, my mouth twisted, in the end I just managed to groan 'Hi', trying to make it sound casual.

The two women stood there, mute, their eyes staring with disbelief. The manservant was behind them: he locked the door. 'I found these two,' he stammered. I had an idea. Making a massive effort I guided my hand towards the sheet and lifted it. The two prostitutes could see my plastic underpants, my crippled legs: I was what I was. 'Filthy pig!' one of the two women, a menacing and colourless blonde, said to the manservant. The other, her hair dyed red, continued the aggression; she exploded in shrieks and swearwords, whirling her bag in the air to hit the unfortunate servant on the back.

'You scummy ugly pig! I'll show you!' she yelled, and much worse besides. Our encounter degenerated into a real street brawl. I was hugely entertained: at first I, too, yelled curses at the women and the servant, indistinctly, then started laughing with my unpleasant voice: I laughed at all the madness, I laughed at my shame. My father knocked at the door, and since the servant didn't dare open up, he threatened to kick it in. Then one of the women turned the key in the lock and my father appeared all ruffled and frothing at the mouth.

'What are you doing here?' he murmured. 'Did you do this? Did you dare do this?' he went on, then stopped himself.

With a lordly gesture he drew two banknotes from his trouser pocket and handed them to the two women. With great courtesy he asked them to go, and hardly had the servant led them away than he hissed between his lips: 'Stop testing us.' Then he pulled out the belt from his trousers and waved it in the air: 'Never test us again.'

'Go away from here,' I said. I don't know whether I was spurred on by courage or hatred. 'The two of us can't live under the same roof. I'm an adult. I do whatever I like.'

'As long as I'm supporting you, you can't do what you want.'

'Then have me cured in an institution. Or throw me out into the street. Would you be brave enough, with all the money you've pilfered? You owe it to me to support me for ever, because you've brought me into the world like this and reduced me to this, with Mama's complicity.'

'You're an intelligent boy: man has a spirit that lifts him above the animals. You can study, I'll help you any way I can. You might become a great mathematician, a philosopher, an artist. Don't limit yourself to being nothing but a cynical loafer just because you're the way you are. Think how many poor people would like to study and are unable to. You still have time to be a great man.'

Poverty and illness, the connection suddenly flashed into my mind. I calmed down and talked to him, with sadness, I remember.

'Please, find somewhere else to live and don't come

here again. We're never going to agree. I'm sorry. We haven't found a way of living together in peace.'

He couldn't make up his mind to go, he seemed nailed to the door-frame.

'Go!' I shouted. 'Let me live alone in this house and I promise I'll study. I'll study the most useless thing that anyone can study: philosophy.'

The next day my father moved to a little villa in which he kept all the precious books he had acquired over the decades in the most expensive antique book markets. He buried himself among his books and I, at the age of eighteen, was left in charge of a miserable self that I didn't know what to do with.

4

I studied.

Now I was no longer in that lair of adolescents all devoted to masturbation, which was what school had been for me, but among young people incubating something indefinable, what Plato calls 'ideas'. They attached themselves to these with passion, suffering, wild determination. 'Ideas', those entities considered eternal, having a real existence outside our brain-cells, entered me. Suddenly, during the first month of study, my fate was decided. Fate! Another very indefinable concept. What am I supposed to do with myself? What am I supposed to do? I wondered during those days of solitude, left in the hands of servants, drivers, cooks and . . . myself. I rolled around the house in my wheelchair asking myself those questions while, crashing into chairs and wardrobes, I tried to shatter my father's knick-knacks. Every now and again I brayed my long, unbridled laugh, deriding myself and fate.

My fate appeared to me one November morning in the darkest corridor of the faculty of letters and philosophy. From a distance I saw something pale moving in the dusk. Outside, a troubling wind was whistling between the trees and little courtyards. I was waiting for my chauffeur. The pale thing was getting closer; I pressed the button on my wheelchair to go towards it. It stopped a few yards away from me. It was a girl's face. A black coat hid the rest of her body. My limbs began to stir: I noticed something disturbing in that face and that darkness. It was a face of a whiteness that I had never seen before: illuminated by its light, red curly hair floated around it. A whispered, slightly husky voice emerged from the face and said: 'Do you have a light, please?' I fell into a panic. But after a moment I understood the meaning of the words. A light for her cigarette! I blushed, felt the blood flowing to my cheeks, my arms began to twitch and whirl more than ever before. I don't know how I did it, but I finally managed to get my lighter out of a little leather bag I always carried with me. I had become an inveterate smoker at university. When I handed her the lighter with its little flame ready, a hand as white as her face, coming suddenly out of the darkness, made its way slowly towards my wrist and calmly gripped it, closing its fingers around it. I felt the warmth of that hand entering me and becoming an excitement that I had never felt before. 'Thank you very much,' the face whispered. I can say today that I experienced then the most beautiful moment of my life. As if the fire of life had penetrated me only then, as if I was born at that moment.

'Really, it's nothing,' I managed to mumble. 'Goodbye,' said the voice. After settling on my wrist, the white hand detached itself and moved towards my face, which it stroked for a moment. I was so moved by the tenderness of the gesture that I started crying. I didn't know how to control myself and then, to do something casual, I murmured a stupid 'Bye'. A moment later the girl was on her way and disappeared into the darkness of the corridor. I stayed there, thinking about her and swearing to do everything possible to see her again. It would be a long time before that happened, but I found another occupation which relieved the pain of waiting and Dora's absence. No, it was not study that distracted me from the thought of her. Knowledge cannot erase feelings. Feelings! Where do they live? In the brain, in the glands, in the blood, the lungs, where, where? How can we define them? How can we speak of them? With the help of Dr F. I tried to plumb the origin of those mysterious things, but in vain. The writings of the philosophers I studied told me nothing. All I know is that from that afternoon my life had changed.

At university I discovered what it meant to belong to a civil society. Yes, my whole being learned to become part of a vast multitude of my peers, if I can put it that way. By dint of travelling, I was in a position to know practically the whole of living humanity. I had journeys arranged around all the continents; my servants and a kind of secretary undertook to plan, map in hand, tours that took me further and further from the city where I was born, away from Europe, to countries with which I was unfamiliar, among people with different languages, customs, food. Sometimes, I can say without any hesitation, the sole purpose of my journey was to find actual slave-girls who would satisfy that instinct that wouldn't leave me in peace. Thus my 'initiation' took place in a sumptuous brothel in a country in the Far East, thanks to the really quite complex work of some girls who held me still, calmed me down and excited me all at the same time. They acted with such skill and grace as to make me think that all men were like me, and that everyone should be treated, the first time, exactly as I was being treated at that moment. It is also true, though, that not everyone would have been in a position to pay as I could, since I was sparing with neither money nor gifts. They were poor girls, and from them I learned the meaning of poverty, the humiliations to which a human being can be driven. Amongst other things, a conspicuous proportion of the inhabitants of those far-off countries lived in appalling conditions, as I observed when being transported to the most densely populated districts, to hovels that I cannot describe with words, tone of voice or gestures.

'This is where man comes from!' I said to myself. 'This is the misery we're hurled into!'

I felt solidarity with that wretched, suffering mass, of which I too was part, although my suffering was of a different kind. I gradually persuaded myself to represent the condition of oppressed man, and told myself that it was my duty to change that condition.

That year the whole planet was shaken by a furious revolutionary movement. The few fellow students with whom I had taken up at university invited me to their meetings, which were increasingly noisy and violent. For the first time in many years, I took part in a demonstration in the square, not, this time, in defence of the homeland and the individual, but for the rights of workers and students. I saw shots being fired (and jumped like a puppet at each impact), people running, cars full of armed police. Once again, as years before, the smoke choked me and again I began to wheeze and cough until I almost fainted. But now everything stirred me and I wanted to feel the same awful sensations every time, if that was what was required in the struggle of the weak and the oppressed.

During one of those demonstrations I saw Dora again. She was in the midst of the crowd and her white face was screaming along with the rest of us. I understood that I would be seeing her often. I felt a sense of happiness, and in the smoke-filled square, in the middle of the fleeing people, I started to spin crazily around in my wheelchair. It was my dance of victory over life's cruelty.

I gradually became the most inflexible revolutionary in the whole faculty. I planned actions of intimidation, I wrote proclamations, hid members of the group that I helped to finance with a small amount of money. Dora was a poor girl and began to come to my house along with her friends. There were about ten of them and they ate in my villa every day, attended to by servants. Sometimes they did the cooking and ate their food sitting on the floor, as in a bivouac. One day, during one of these 'meetings', my father arrived. I hadn't seen him for months. He looked terribly drawn and tired. He stopped on the threshold of the drawing-room, which was a confusion of clothes, waste paper, dirty plates. Without saying a word, my father took a sheet of paper from his pocket. He gave it to me with hands trembling. It was a warrant for my arrest.

'What have you done? What are you planning on doing?' he asked.

'Defend me! That's why you're a lawyer,' I answered. I wasn't afraid. I felt intoxicated as only a man who is blindly obsessed can feel.

'Who are these gentlemen?'

'Are you going to spy on us? Look at him, guys! He's a filthy spy!' I said with my tremulous sheep's voice.

'Take him away from here. If they find him I won't be able to get him out of jail,' my father whispered. After a brief consultation they carried me away in their arms. Outside, my father's car was ready and waiting. They drove me to the hills, to an abandoned house. It was there that we planned the kidnapping of an American diplomat.

5

We had been studying for months. The isolated house on the windswept upland plain became our general head-quarters. We slept there ten or twenty at a time, in heavy-duty sleeping-bags, in the acrid smell of smoke. We prepared our plan down to the tiniest details. Not even I knew which day had been selected to put the project into action. I learned the result from the newspapers and the radio. Attempts were begun to rescue the prisoner. We set very difficult conditions: the liberation of some of our comrades, a considerable sum of money to be paid for his ransom, maximum publicity for the event. We were waiting for the reply. It was evening. We had put out the lights. That was a necessary precaution. We were afraid of an attack by the police. We were sitting on the floor, no one said a word. Dora was beside me. She took out a cig-arette, looked around, then brought her face close to me and asked me for a light.

'Got a match?'

She turned to the others. 'Who's going to give me a light?'

No one moved. I took my lighter out of my bag and held it out to her, the little flame already lit.

At that moment a burst of machine-gun fire rang out from outside and an agitated voice shouted at us to surrender. It all happened in an instant. One boy threw a grenade through the window, there was an extremely loud explosion, other grenades flew, mad shooting broke out, and in the confusion I clutched Dora, clutched her breast. I didn't want to die without feeling she was united with me. The next moment I was lifted up and carried away through a side door. Fortunately I was short of breath, and an epileptic fit deprived me of consciousness. I woke up in a car travelling at terrifying speed, and behind us was another with its sirens blaring. Someone pressed my hand around a revolver and made me pull the trigger: the shot gave me a violent jolt, I started back as though I had been shot myself. The car behind us burst into flames and once again a fit obscured everything from my mind. But I was left with the memory of having killed some human beings.

I found myself on the ground in the garden of the villa. It took me a moment or two to recognize it. My father was crouching beside me. He was trying to lift me off the ground. Stumbling he managed to carry me into the house. The chauffeur took delivery of me, carried me up the stairs, undressed me, washed me, dressed me in my pyjamas and put me in my bed. Half an hour later the police dragged me from it, taking me straight to solitary confinement. A week later my father managed to get me put on house arrest: without all the treatment I needed I could have died at any moment, and if that happened the judge would have been guilty of deliberate homicide. The trial lasted three months. Acting out a laborious opera of persuasion, resorting to arguments that were incomprehensible to me but clearly effective, my father managed to get me acquitted.

'You aren't a murderer, you can't be,' he said to me one evening.

'Even if I were, you'd have to defend me anyway. You condemned me to be what I am. You! You did!'

'I know. You're innocent, I know that.'

I gave up arguing: what did he know about innocence and guilt? In my eyes, at that time, he was the rich bastard and that was that. He was thinner every time I saw him, but always more convinced of my innocence. I told him only a small part of what I knew, I didn't trust him, the callous, wealthy bourgeois, the exploiter without an ideal to his name. But I had to admire the tenacity and bravado with which he constructed his masterpiece as a lawyer. My acquittal, or perhaps merely the end of the trial, left him depressed. Not only his career but his whole life came to an end with that trial. He had a malignant tumour in his throat and it might be said that he spoke his address with the last breath in his body. In getting me acquitted, he had also performed the task of his life. He came to get me, sat down in an armchair, very smartly dressed, like a guest: he didn't want to consider the villa his home, this man who had arrived in the country without a penny and worked for so many years to grow rich. He showed me the list of all the movable and immovable goods, gave me the numbers of current accounts he was leaving to me, stocks, shares; he talked to me, in a reedy voice, of all the precious books scattered around the various houses; all in all, he explained to me that he had worked only to ensure that I had a comfortable life, a steady source of income. Then he started crying.

'Which of the two of us is the more wretched?' he asked, sobbing. I couldn't pretend.

'I am,' I said firmly.

'No. It's me. Me,' he whispered. 'That's the worst sentence. Having to die. Why?'

'Papa. You can't go on living for ever.'

'Why? Tell me why I can't?'

'Everything is consumed. Everything will end up in the gigantic pyre of the universe, in chaos and disorder. Matter is not eternal.'

'But something must be. Something must be eternal.'

'Do you want to make a drama of yourself again?' I asked, as gently as I could manage.

'Yes. Do you have any objections?'

What could I say to a dying man? A sentence occurred to me, one that I had never thought of before. And yet I said it to him sincerely, and with tears in my eyes: 'Papa. In the end I love you. I always have done.' My arms started to flounder, my legs began to kick. I saw the poor old man, his whole body shaking with emotion. He died of a heart attack, half an hour later.

6

The most painful part of the farce was over. No one would ever torture me again, knee me in the spine to make me walk, hang me from the wall-bars to lengthen me, no one would ask me to speak, think, study, devote myself to goodness, animated by feelings of goodness. I was alone, rich and free. Freedom! What a difficult word. I had shouted it hundreds of times, I had claimed absolute freedom in public speeches and rhythmical choral shouts, I had studied it in dozens of books and maintained the idea in the face of presumptuous professors. But now, by the grave into which I was to lower my father's body, I felt like that Umbrian saint who saw herself suspended in the void. In the face of death, the great sentiment of solidarity no longer pushed my wheelchair, it didn't stop the uncontrollable agitation of my limbs. I felt pain, rage and despair. Then, beneath the pitilessly falling snow, opposite me, on the other side of the grave, I saw Dora's face once again. 'There she is, she'll be my salvation,' I thought, and while they were cutting my white shirt at the level of my heart as a sign of penitence, someone shouted after the coffin which was descending into the earth, the ritual phrase: 'Remember you're dead!' Looking at that white, white face, I tried to communicate not my will, this time, but a desolate request.

It is difficult for me to know how Dora replied that day. I thought I recognized a sign in her expression, as if she too wanted to harpoon me with that nebulous thing, the language of the eyes. As the ceremony drew towards its conclusion, I pushed my wheelchair towards her, going around the tomb which was by now completely covered. I bleated my dull and stupid 'Hi', and she hugged me and kissed me on the eyes. What did the gesture mean? Maternal affection? Intimacy? An invitation not to look to the bottom of things, to follow my fate with my eyes closed? I thought about this all night, gradually emptying a whole bottle of whisky. I was at home! I was free! I could do whatever I wanted! I wanted to do something with her, with Dora. Towards dawn I called her on the phone, begging her to join me. Speaking ambiguously, I led her to believe that there was a political secret at stake. And so, at the first light of dawn, she came. I had wanted to see her for so long, and finally there she was. She sat down on the floor as she always had done at meetings. She took out a cigarette and I was about to reach for my lighter, but this time she had some matches. She refused my light with a shake of her head, then turned towards me with a harshness that I would never have expected.

'Who did you betray to stay out of jail?'

My whole body gave a start; my arms, my legs and my neck stirred into motion in an instant, my eyes rolled back, I puffed and wheezed alarmingly, until, making a huge effort, I managed to rattle off the worst, most vulgar words I had ever uttered, the most obscene expletives the human mind can think of. Accusing me of such baseness was a mortal offence, a slander, but nonetheless I should never have railed at her like that! Railing at my love! I realized this a moment later, while I was still shrieking, but it was too late. I couldn't retract a word of it. To have asked forgiveness would have made things worse, so I doubled the dose, spitting out even more poison and filthy saliva at the only person I had ever loved in my whole life.

Loved? What is love? Can you contemplate the rubbish that was issuing from my brain, from my soul? Yes, my soul! Because in the midst of that filth, that garbage, something was beginning to appear, something that is not only desire, instinct, matter, but something else, something that belongs only to man, and I don't know what it can be. But I felt it at the same time as I was yelling at her, dreadful vulgarities with which I will not burden the reader's imagination. I became aware of it within me, at that very wretched moment. But from now on I was lost. I had sentenced myself to dangle in the void, like a hanged man, who cannot die but chokes for eternity.

After a few minutes I stopped and looked at her, wheezing as though I was about to burst. I don't know why I didn't suffer an epileptic attack, as I had before in similar situations. Dora got up and extinguished her cigarette.

'Anyway, I'll soon know the truth,' she said and left. In order to go with her I thought of hurling myself down the stairs, I certainly couldn't get down them in my wheelchair, but Dora had already disappeared. I saw the flash of light when the front door opened and closed, I heard the booming thud that seemed to announce my death.

What could I do to make good that dreadful mistake? I called my manservant, had him undress me and went to sleep. I accepted that I was a monster in my soul and my body, and I began to feel innocent, as my father had said I was. An innocent monster, just like our century . . .

I spent day after day drinking whisky, smoking and stuffing myself with the food that I ordered up from the best restaurants in the city. I didn't dare call anyone, because I knew that any conversation I had would be recorded by the police. I didn't know how to track down Dora, who changed her address every day. I spent a number of years like that, trying to help, with money and legal aid, all my friends who were forced to go into hiding.

I hated my wealth. If I hadn't been as I was, I would have thrown it all away: money, possessions, works of art.

But I wanted to live and, given my condition, in order to live one had to be rich. In the animal world my peers would have devoured me long ago, and I would have eased their hunger for a number of days. Mankind let me live, but I had to pay for my life with ready cash, buying a few expensive moments. I decided to deprive myself of nothing. I sold the books. The books, those works of the human spirit, on a single one of which, on occasion, whole civilizations had been built, now seemed dispensable. I no longer wanted to read. What for? To become more erudite, more spiritual, more religious, to amuse myself, to masturbate? There were much easier ways of doing all those things. I entered the savage ranks of today's potential illiterates. I sold precious manuscripts, antique volumes, miniature parchments, rare editions of monumental works (including a first edition of Voltaire's *Encyclopédie*). I attended sales in London, New York and Tokyo and witnessed the exorbitant sums that certain individuals obsessed by those trifles were willing to shell out. My braying became famous in the rooms of Christies' and Sotheby's; when they saw me turning up in the arms of my chauffeur or in my wheelchair, I chilled the spines of those seasoned jackals of other people's misery. In that way I freed myself for good of all the books, and went on tanning myself, smoking, having myself carried around the brothels of the Far and the Near East. But I had my obsession: a feeling.

Feelings are the things that have always filled novels,

and continue to fill them today, to draw a tear, a wide-eyed dream that lasts a second or two, to transform each tear, each dreaming moment into money. The Scriptures have had their day. Now that youth is past, I no longer feel any enthusiasm for the future: sometimes I lose heart, I think insistently of suicide. Why aren't we swept away by a comet erupting from some distant corner of the universe? Why doesn't the whole material world collapse? That way, apart from the little daily farce, the great comedy of the universe, the representation of everything, would also come to an end. But I still want to tell the story of the most stirring part of my life: the universal sap, the real diversion. And to whom is this part of the story linked if not to the person of Dora and my 'feeling' for her?

7

After many years spent turning her around in my head, I found her again. It was a May morning, by chance, while I was looking in the window of an antique shop in the old town. Turning my wheelchair to go, I ran into that white face and black coat, as though time had stopped. I started laughing with joy, with my mocking, braying, spittle-filled laugh, and she smiled with her gleaming eyes and her sulky child's mouth. 'So something, somebody does exist!' I thought, and tears came to my eyes as my hoarse sheep's voice repeated, 'Dora, Dora, Dora.' She didn't say anything, but stared at me, and I thought I discerned a vague promise in her expression. That game lasted perhaps five minutes, then my Mercedes arrived and brought us both home. There was no longer any sense in pretending, in stopping myself. I invited her to sit in a comfortable chair. She took off her coat. Without her coat she was much more beautiful than I had ever seen her before, at the political meetings.

I told her I loved her. I repeated it in my comical way, my whole face contorted with embarrassment, and then I said it a third time, puffing and spluttering like an old locomotive.

She smiled and murmured, 'Really?' sounding incredulous and somehow intimate.

I hissed 'Yes'. She took out her cigarette and I lit it.

'Well then, what are we going to do?' she said after five minutes of silence.

'I don't know. I swear I don't know,' I said. 'Do you know?'

'I've never thought about it.'

'Do you have to? Thought doesn't come into such things,' I managed to blurt out.

'Do you mean that?' Dora asked. 'So what does?'

'Well, things like . . .' Things that led inexorably towards other ways of conceiving the world, other ways of acting, different from the ones that had brought us together in the years before. I remained silent.

'Do you mean the instincts?' Dora asked, with a broad and enigmatic smile. I still said nothing. I was uneasy. What instincts could draw her towards me? All of a sudden Dora got to her feet and came close to me.

'We'll meet here tomorrow at five. You send your chauffeur and your manservant away. It has to stay a secret. Can you open the door on your own?'

I stammered that I had every automatic gadget imaginable, then laughed with my usual laugh, and she put her black coat back on, said goodbye with a little pat on my cheek and left.

I didn't sleep, I didn't eat, I didn't think either that night or the following morning: my whole being was stirring within me in an indescribable, inexplicable way. Something other than instinct. I spent the whole morning and part of the afternoon engaging in ludicrous preparations: I tried out perfumes, flowers, drinks – changed them and changed them again. The staff left me on my own. No one turned up at five o'clock, or at six. At half-past six the doorbell rang, and I pressed the buttons so hard that the device jammed. I had to call the fire brigade to open the gate and the front door. By the time the whole fuss was over, it was already time for Dora to go. Because I couldn't send the whole staff off duty, we postponed the appointment for a week. I spent those days resorting to sleeping tablets and alcohol, and was prey to a boundless appetite: anxiety forced me to ingest huge quantities.

'If you go on fattening yourself up like that, I'm quitting,' the chauffeur said clearly and bluntly. 'I've no intention of giving myself a hernia lifting you up and putting you back down in the car.'

I kept myself in check for the final two days, and then came the date of the new appointment. I was left on my own and this time Dora was on time. It was the last week in May, she no longer needed her coat: she was wearing a beautiful tight, low-cut dress. The sight of her took my breath away. She sat down opposite me on a sofa and started talking.

'I've had plenty of time to think. What would you like from me?' she said straight out. I was uneasy again.

'You know very well that it's terribly complicated for me to have the things I'd like. I beg your forgiveness.'

'What for? You'd be better off concentrating on what it is that you'd like and what you can really have,' she said calmly. I was constantly agitated. I thought I was going to die on the spot. I wondered whether love made everyone suffer as much, why that was the way things were when it was all just a pointless torment. In my confusion I was unable to find an answer.

'Do you want me to be with you day and night?' she asked.

'No! No! Please! No!' I was terrified that she might be disgusted with me, with my intimacy.

'Do you want me to be close to you, like an inseparable friend?'

'Yes! I'd love that.'

'So you want me as a friend, love doesn't come into it?'

'Yes! It is love. I don't know what to do. I'm desperate. I want to kill myself!' I squealed with my nasal voice. 'You kill me! Go on, kill me! There must be a gun in that box over there.'

'Calm down,' she said, 'calm down.' I was nothing but a wheezing noise, a ceaseless agitation. She remained silent and motionless and I became gradually calmer. Then, without saying a word, Dora opened the top part of her floral dress and revealed herself as naked as the day she was born. I was hypnotized. I was trembling.

'I thought I would do that, for now. That and nothing more.' She stayed that way for about ten minutes, looking at me in silence, smoking her cigarette. I looked at her smooth white skin, her breasts, now less full than before, her beautiful broad shoulders, and I repeated her name, unable to do anything else. After a while Dora put her clothes back on, stroked my hair, kissed me on the cheek and, without saying goodbye or anything else, went away. I was sure I would never see her again.

The months passed. By the time the wind swept through our city, the sea was black and I thought each morning of how I could put an end to my life, one night at midnight my manservant woke me up, furiously announcing that a lady had been ringing at the door. She wanted to see me and talk to me. He told me her name. It was Dora. Panicking, I told him to bring her in immediately but I didn't know what attitude to adopt, whether to get dressed, to wash, to comb my hair, or just to receive her as I was, with the stink of alcohol and smoke and the stench of grease that had stayed on me from the pub where I had spent the evening. The anxiety of seeing Dora again was so great that in the end I had her sent straight up to my room.

'Forgive me for disturbing you at this time of night,' she murmured, dropping into an armchair.

'Stop joking. You're giving me a wonderful present. Without you I wanted to die.'

'Really?' said the husky, whispering voice I knew so well.

'Yes,' I wheezed. My arms were jerking around. I couldn't sit still. 'Yes, I wanted to die. Happy the man for whom the hour of his death is like that of his birth. I read that last week. *Bersiyath 4d*. At the moment of my birth they squashed my head, you see. I want to have my head squashed again when I died. To be happy. To be happy.'

Dora started laughing. 'Stop it. You can still be happy while you're alive.' She grew serious. She said nothing for a few minutes, then she rose to her feet. 'I'd thought of something else, the last time we saw each other. Then events made me go into hiding. Now I'm going to put that thought into action.'

Without continuing she looked at me, then she undressed completely and remained motionless in front of me. 'That's what I thought. All I did was think of you during those months,' she whispered. 'Do you want me to turn round?'

I looked at her, listening to the pulse in my veins and my breath going like a piston. I was excited, but what disturbed me the most was not yearning and instinct, but the vision of beauty. I had never seen anything more harmonious in a living creature. Perhaps it was all down to education, what I had been taught at school, art, the transformation of my instinct into contemplation. The whiteness of the slender figure, that November night, seemed to me something so invincible that I closed my eyes.

'Do you want to smell me?' said Dora's voice, and I didn't dare open my eyes, nor my mouth to speak. Gradually I heard my chest giving out that terrible wheezing noise that was my breath. I couldn't hold it back. Dora was right: I could still be happy, in life. I shook, I wriggled about, I wept without restraint or shame. Then, within me, a terrible force was unleashed: instinct. I hurled myself at Dora with my wheelchair. Dora fled with a shriek. Furniture was overturned, glass was broken. I followed her all around the room: it was my struggle with the angel, with grace, with the Presence. I grabbed her, she began to drag me around and still I wouldn't let go. I fell out of the wheelchair, which turned over. Crawling, I clutched her legs and was pulled around like that, shrieking. In the end she freed herself and ran to pick up her belongings. When I reopened my eyes, Dora was already dressed and combing her hair. She was frightened.

'I hope I didn't hurt you,' she said quietly.

'No,' I managed to say.

'I have so many things to tell you. I came here because I haven't got anywhere to live. Sorry for disturbing you.'

'You have nowhere to live? Why didn't you tell me before?'

'Because I had a place to live before.'

I offered her one of my apartments, I was happy to be able to do something for her. She refused.

'I'm not asking for anything in exchange. Nothing. Don't worry about that,' I hurried to say.

'Let's see tomorrow,' said Dora. 'I'm off now. I'll decide when to give myself to you. Let's not test each other any more.'

'Where are you going?' I asked, very worried. She seemed at ease.

'I'm not down and out. Not having somewhere to live isn't the end of the world. Far from it. I'm staying with a girlfriend at the moment. I'll be in touch.'

She left. 'Don't wait six months before coming back!' I yelled, but I don't know if she heard.

I was alone again. I was all daubed with blood, with an arm and a leg seared with pain. They were both broken. I had to have myself taken to casualty. I was in plaster for three months. I was alone. Who could I confide in? Who could I ask for advice or help? Dora might be some kind of adventurer, I didn't know much about her. But one thing was important. Happiness still existed on earth, this century could close with the vision of beauty and grace, it wasn't all selfishness, vulgarity, meaninglessness. You just had to wait. The next day Dora didn't come. Or the day after.

What was to be done? Part of my life was driving me back towards pubs and brothels, to assert the triumph of the ego, of meaninglessness and the void. The other part, as happens to all men, told me to find a purpose: give away what I possessed, get rid of everything, degrade myself completely, be in poverty and in need, but be useful to someone. It's also the choice of the age I live in. Which of these two tendencies do you think won out in me?

8

It isn't easy to say. I waited for Dora to come back, because by now I was sure she would. I didn't know where to look for her, how to look for her, but I was sure she would come, and with her presence all my ills – the blind groping, the epilepsy, the pessimism – would disappear. Dora had shown herself in all her beauty and that beauty would never again abandon me. I waited patiently. I had once again started reading books that I bought in antique shops, I listened to music and dabbled in some speculations on the stock market with the shares of a big insurance company; hardly had I bought them than the shares started increasing in value, adding money to what I already possessed. Evidently fate looked kindly upon me. But Dora had disappeared. Gradually my waiting turned to anguish. 'She's deceived me. She's never coming back. She's going to leave me in this misery, in this uncertainty,' I thought. I was beginning not to be able to distinguish between a longing for her beauty and the desire to return to those filthy hovels, in the midst of degraded humanity, in bestiality's lair.

'Why don't we go off on a nice journey like we used to?' my secretary asked me one day. 'The world is big, bigger than you think.'

I agreed. 'Yes, travelling, getting away from myself. Dying among strangers, as a stranger. That strikes me as the solution.'

I ordered my secretary to organize journeys across all the continents, so that I would see the world before I died. I thought that in the confusion of flight I would cancel out my thoughts, my feelings. As everyone knows, our yearning to predict the future is ridiculous and the first stop was enough to make a mockery of it. I was in Mexico City, among the twenty million inhabitants of that organic agglomeration when, one day, passing through the district called Judia, I saw something incredibly white coming towards me. It was Dora, wearing a light dress the colour of her skin! My heart leaped, but my limbs also moved so abruptly as to hurt my muscles. I don't know how I survived that moment.

I started calling her in a loud voice, a number of times: quite useless in the monstrous hubbub of the city. Dora passed close by without noticing me. I went on calling her and my chauffeur yelled as well, but in the course of a few seconds the white figure was swallowed up by the crowd. I felt I was going mad. I thought of her voice, her figure, her skin, her hair: unfortunately I couldn't remember her perfume. And to think that months before I had started to weep like an idiot rather than taking advantage of her proximity, her nudity, the love she had declared in no uncertain terms. I had let her go for fear of my monstrosity.

I put calls through to all the hotels in Mexico City, we looked for her in clubs and bars (by now I thought of her as a down-and-out), naturally to no avail. I continued my flight. In Tokyo something similar happened to the incident in Mexico. I imagined I saw her, and my chauffeur also swore blind that it was she, but once again Dora disappeared without leaving a trace. Was it possible that it was all an illusion? That my desire to see her again had communicated itself to the chauffeur, and that the two of us together, with our imaginations, were creating Dora's presence? When the same thing happened for the third time, in Nairobi, I told my chauffeur and my secretary to cancel the other stops on the journey and bring me back home. I understood that I could not escape my destiny.

And what is that destiny? I don't know. All I know is that I will have to flounder as long as I live, unable to command my gestures, both torturer and tortured, both a condemned man and the instrument of my own execution. But I have glimpsed Beauty, I have glimpsed the 'right-hand side', what can I do if I escape, if she obsesses me first with her presence and then with her absence? What must I do, tell me, unknown recipient of this message . . . given that I manage to reach you . . . You are like me, we are both more or less defective pieces on the conveyor belt, and sooner or later you will be discarded.

This is my story. I wanted to leave a trace of it. But by now everything that is said or written is in discredit, if it is not transformed into money. As the illustrious linguist Pinker says, 'all discourse is pure illusion'.

So, in simple words, the simplest possible, I have written my testament, leaving all my goods to Dora. The lawyer has the task of finding her. He will look for her, on my behalf, everywhere. He, too, will, if necessary, spend his whole life looking for her. By now I too think the same way as most of the inhabitants of this continent: the list of my goods is the sole text in which I now place any trust. I have countersigned it with the stamp I inherited from my father.

Now I am here, in the drawing room of my sumptuous villa. All I do is eat, I have put on four stone and my chauffeur has resigned. I haven't found a new one yet. I breathe with difficulty, my stomach prevents the movement of my diaphragm. I suffer from catarrh. My head is spinning. I am afraid that I will soon lose consciousness. Throughout my life I have tried everything. I have had no certainty. A shame. I have lived dissolutely, I have killed, but nonetheless perhaps my father was right, perhaps I am innocent. Can you grasp the meaning of that word yet? I hope so.

The end

THE PURSUIT

I received this story when the present volume had already
been set and was about to go to press. The text reached
me via fax. It is a piece of writing by my dearest former
classmate, my brother. He was a mild-mannered boy,
quiet but with a great inner clarity, an even temper and a
good disposition towards others which I only now fully
understand and appreciate. Two nights ago I dreamed
about him. And today, in reply, here is this manuscript. A
strange coincidence. The fax comes from Milan. My
brother Nicola has not been with us for twelve years.
These pages were found at the bottom of a drawer where
they lay in the midst of other personal objects. I felt that
the dark stories assembled in this volume needed some
concluding lightness. For that reason I have asked the
publisher to add this story at the last moment.

I

She's a witch, I tell you. She tangles the fate of men, alive and dead. I know I am one of her creations, moulded by her in flesh and spirit: I have been sleeping with her for many years. The elements themselves, air and earth, sun and water, help her in her work. Otherwise you would have to believe in a will capable of conquering the deadly inertia of matter and bending to its own designs space, events, time.

I remember when I first saw her, opening her heavy lids, emerging from the void. I met her blue eyes, her little face. I looked at the lines of her slender body, her coloured socks, the little shoes – children's shoes almost, with buckles and little straps – her long hair. I looked at her hands. Her smile, too, was a child's.

That's how I want you to remember her as well: a pale lunar light that love has rendered clairvoyant and armed with extraordinary powers, sending it out across the whole world before finding me, and bringing me back to life.

She was twenty-five and already married when all of a sudden she fell in love. Some of the things I shall now confide in you I heard from the lips of Vittoria herself, some from her acquaintances and old friends. I want you to know everything, you men who have lived but once.

She was twenty-five, I was saying. And although she was a girl, she had studied philosophy and theology. The long hours spent on her books had turned her even paler. An orphan – her father had died many years before – she had received thoughts and suggestions from Plato and his heirs, she had examined the fate of Boethius and Descartes, of faded mystics and preachers. They had become her fathers. She knew of the world beyond, that world that no hand can touch nor any eye see, which exists in the thoughts of all of us. I am talking about ideas, of that state of our mental machinery, running from person to person, which hangs over, or seems to hang over, our common fates. Not that she believed in them: the professors, with their arguments of logic and history, had not instilled them into her with any conviction. It was Greek philosophy itself that spoke to and seduced her. And Vittoria had bent her head before the words of the fathers. Closing her eyes, she managed to see the world above and, between that and the palpable real world, she sensed yet other spaces, other beings, other lives.

In the dark rooms of the university, where many sunsets surprised her, behind the shelves of books, above the gaze of her companions, unknown yet familiar presences revealed themselves.

Giovanni, the young assistant who married Vittoria as soon as she had finished her university studies, had sensed nothing. But, disagreeable as it might be to admit it, her philosophy teacher, the favourite disciple of the professor, who was a luminary of phenomenology during those years in Milan, embodied, more than pure thought, 'brute reality', to use the exact phrase.

Lavish dinners with friends, healthy swims in the sea and in pools, a protective paternal presence: that was what the young professor Giovanni offered Vittoria. It seemed like a promise for all eternity. 'A little Eldorado,' she said later, with a laugh. Because, in all of this she could find nothing but a source of laughter.

Even when she was united in matrimony before the civil world, as embodied by the municipal functionary, she was really laughing loud and long in her heart. Her joyfulness conveyed itself to her future father-in-law, a respectable businessman, the witnesses – serious university teachers – and all the guests.

There was laughter as they signed the register; and even while the married couple and their guests were going down the stairs of the building and pouring into the street to part shortly afterwards, a resonant good humour insinuated its way among them.

But the laughter was not a sign of happiness. Vittoria soon discovered that the union of her body with that of Giovanni was only a cause of pain. She spent anguished nights beside her husband wishing him as far away as possible. A few weeks after the wedding she began to take sleeping tablets and when her husband lay down beside her Vittoria, almost unconscious, turned to face the other way.

I realize that my words are running ahead of me. I am

crossing time and space, indicating few and inadequate details. I should be speaking about Giovanni, saying that he was remarkably tall, well-off, with coarse manners despite his studies. I should bring you into the couple's house, talk about the furniture, the curtains, the bed, their thoughts, their night-time conversations, their feelings. I haven't time to do that. The story of Vittoria's love is here in my breast and in my thoughts, it doesn't leave so much as a page for anyone else. It begs for testimony, and it does so with each passing moment, with the pulsing of my blood, whose very source it is.

Vittoria had been married for a few months when she met a short man, thin, with shaggy hair and big frightened eyes. Giacomo was an art dealer and a painter. The works of many hands were bundled together in his studio. African votive statues were arranged on two tables; they were of various sizes, carved from all kinds of wood. Rather than human creations, they seemed casually sculpted by fate. Their material – wood – had preserved its own nature, and the human figures were superimposed upon it, something pallid and accidental.

Man and tree, two beings were united to represent one another: wood stood for man, and man for wood.

A little further along, mannequins made by Italian craftsmen some centuries back, an aid for painters and designers, showed their painted pink cheeks and stared at certain corners of the room. In their material, the wood was no longer recognizable: they were artificial creatures, neither flesh nor tree, they sat there motionlessly with no precise reason for their existence. Perhaps Giacomo was seeking the union of two worlds in some of his painted woods. Or perhaps over time he had realized that he himself was incapable of effecting that union whose concept remained with him in the form of an *idée fixe*. Many of his pictures were clusters of knots: pieces of string tied together and then cut and then tied and cut again. He had spent months making knots, alone in his studio, among his mannequins.

Do I think that Vittoria had noticed this anxious quest for connections the evening she found herself in the artist-dealer's studio along with her friends and acquaintances? Or perhaps I think this because I now know that she has been on the same quest as long as she has lived. However, the encounter was a revelation for her.

'In this lift we had our first kiss.

'In front of this shop window we kissed once, when he had to leave for America.

'I sat on this bench weeping.' That was what Vittoria would say to me each time we crossed the city on apparently casual trajectories.

The man didn't notice her immediately. It was the girl who made the first move.

'I want to marry you and have a child by you,' she said in circumstances that I would describe as exceptional.

Giacomo replied with a fixed expression: 'But I am old and ill.'

Vittoria kissed him. She felt his frail body, his slack muscles. She resolved never to let him go.

By the time the conversation took place Giacomo's life was already marked; it was after Giacomo's journey to Africa, his final one. Its purpose was the acquisition of statuettes, this time without the mediation of international traders, who cared nothing for the souls of those people but a great deal for profit; often they would not refer (perhaps because they were fakes) to the exact provenance of the objects. The flight from Rome to the Sudan was interrupted after three hours when four terrorists burst into the pilot's cabin. They were Arabs. They wanted money. They wanted the deaths of the Jews and an enemy Sheik.

The aircraft remained motionless in a tropical airport. By the time unknown soldiers from a secret police force had climbed up the fuselage and stormed the plane, the passengers were already exhausted. The smoke from a tear-gas canister ripped through Giacomo's lungs before the terrorists were killed.

Another plane brought him back to Italy. His thin body had managed to survive. In hospital Vittoria spent many days beside this man, sitting close to his bed. Giacomo recovered. But slowly, in his lungs, a formless kind of flesh was beginning to grow, the kind that men call 'malignant'.

Perhaps Giacomo's body wanted that growth for reasons that his mind could neither understand nor control. The doctors couldn't understand or control it either. The flesh went on growing inexorably.

It was then that Vittoria and Giacomo were united. Vittoria parted from her husband without hesitation; she watched him weeping like a baby. 'Would it have been better to lie?' she asked. She left him the house and all the objects of her father's inheritance that she had brought with her: furniture, ornaments, paintings.

She and Giacomo moved to Paris, to a little apartment in Saint-Germain-des-Prés. 'We'll live more calmly here,' he had said.

Vittoria, before she left, spoke to a doctor friend. 'Two to four years,' was the sentence.

Nothing happened. Giacomo went on knotting pieces of string; the mannequins and the African statues left their confines in an old car, sitting beside Vittoria, as though they were alive. In the Paris house they were stored in a room all to themselves.

In the evening Giacomo and Vittoria met other painters and other antique dealers. The collection of old and strange objects grew bigger: human limbs in plaster, dolls, figures of animals were added to what was already there. By day she went in search of objects to sell and to preserve.

But now I am becoming aware that I will never manage to tell you what that love was: the little everyday details might seem banal, commonplace, at best attempts to extract some cheap emotion from the situation. The words they exchanged, even if they were quoted faithfully as I have heard them from Vittoria's lips, would be meaningless to an outsider. And how then can one say that two people love each other?

What had seemed a torture to Vittoria with Giovanni, with Giacomo became happiness. In her body it was no longer painful thorns that sprouted at the moment of their union, but sweet flowers, and rather than being absent, she now wanted to be perennially in the presence of her man.

This happiness was too much for Giacomo's frail body; or perhaps it was too much in the judicious eyes of the family doctor.

'I have to prescribe him some tranquillizers or you will wear yourself out,' said Dr Issuna, when Vittoria talked to him of her lover's inextinguishable ardour. They embraced and kissed for hours together, several times a day.

The official prohibition on picking those sweet amorous flowers did no damage to relations between Vittoria and Giacomo. They stayed cheerful even when his coughing, at first timid and sporadic, began to be violent and prolonged.

'I'm being like Violetta in *La Traviata*,' he said, turning away, every time a cough rose to his throat. He smiled. And when the attack had passed his eyes were pearly with tears.

Now it became tiring for Giacomo to make knots in

his pieces of string. '*Parigi o cara noi lasceremo,*' he sang softly, when he had to go back to Milan for treatment.

They decided to marry. Vittoria's marriage to Giovanni had been dissolved very quickly. Dr Issuna went on holiday. He admitted to Vittoria that he was unable to help his friend Giacomo.

'If he's in a lot of pain, here's an injection to give him,' he said and added in a low voice: 'It'll send him to sleep.'

Before the coughing paralysed him, Giacomo went for a walk with Vittoria. They stopped in a meadow to pick flowers and thistles. Giacomo knew the names of every plant in the meadow. He taught them all to Vittoria, one by one. Then, when he was at home again, he went to bed. A few days later, Vittoria could no longer bear the sight of his pain. She gave him the tranquillizing injection. The coughing stopped.

'Why wait a month, we could get married immediately,' he said one afternoon. A neighbour acted as celebrant, some friends as witnesses. The names of Vittoria and Giacomo were knotted together like two pieces of string. Giacomo, for the ceremony, wanted to wear his pyjama jacket. Early that evening he went to sleep. He died, after a year and a half of life and love with Vittoria.

When they put him in the coffin, the girl put beside him a fake ivory hand, from the nineteenth century, for him to stroke, and two wooden African figures: passports on the infinite journeys into other worlds.

II

It is now, with the death of her lover, that Vittoria's fortunes took an extraordinary and admirable turn.

But before speaking of the other men who appeared in her life in rapid succession, I would like to say something more about her, to provide a better understanding either of her love for Giacomo or of what happened afterwards.

Vittoria had been born a girl contrary to the wishes of her parents who, after the birth of their first daughter, Adriana, would have preferred a boy. Her mother, a woman admired for her beauty, did not show excessive love for her; her father preferred the other daughter, the taciturn little sister who meekly allowed herself to be stroked, like a cat. Vittoria, on the other hand, drummed her feet and cried. But the more furiously she demanded love, the more she was repulsed.

At the age of ten, her relatives judged her too strange. Her mother put everything down to a nasty fall in the second year of her life: escaping the arms of the wet-nurse, Vittoria had fallen headlong on to the ground.

Her paternal grandmother, Isis, who came from regions where ancient beliefs had their roots, was of a different opinion. 'That girl has the devil in her body,' she repeated. At this time her father had been dead for more than a year: a mysterious inflammation of the lungs had carried him off in the space of a few weeks, before he could even say goodbye to his daughters and give them his last instructions and advice. Vittoria was unable to see him from the day he was taken to hospital. Only from the words of her grandmother, her aunts and her mother was she able to understand the course of the illness, its aggravation and the approach of the end. It was her mother's weeping, one Sunday morning, that told her of her father's death. Vittoria saw someone coming into her parents' bedroom, picking up her father's smartest suit, his finest tie, red and gold, a white shirt, his black shoes.

'To dress Daddy, who's going off on a very long journey,' her mother said with a sob. By the time the children were brought in, the coffin was already closed and about to be carried shoulder-high from the boiling hospital room to the hearse. Her mother did not have the heart to accompany the coffin; Vittoria saw the black hearse disappearing on the journey that she really thought of as being very long, but not a journey of no return.

At home she wandered around forlornly; the portraits collected by her father looked down on her from the walls, faces that she imagined were those of people he would know and consort with over the course of his journey. The faces were unlike those of everyday people, perhaps of different races, or perhaps from worlds other than the one she knew and experienced daily.

'When is Daddy coming back?' she asked her mother. And she reacted to the incomprehensible replies with furious tears. Or else she closed her eyes, trying to follow her father's journey in her mind's eye, to guess which character from the portraits he was keeping company with at that moment. When that happened she laughed and talked to herself, imagining she was joining in with her father's conversations.

Sometimes, late in the evening, she started awake and got up. She heard whispered words coming from her mother's room; she thought that her mother too was communicating secretly with the dead man. 'No, I'm talking to someone on the telephone,' her mother finally said one day to calm her down, instead provoking a storm of jealousy in the child's heart.

'Believe me, the devil has slipped into her body,' said her grandmother after a prolonged bout of furious weeping by Vittoria. 'What we need is a priest.'

Vittoria was taken to the doctor, undressed, examined on a little bed. She shivered, she felt she was losing her senses as the doctor's hands ran over her body. No physical abnormality was found; not even the insistent questions about what she felt when 'those crises' arrived yielded anything concrete.

'She will grow, and everything will adjust,' was the doctor's verdict.

The exorcist arrived some days later, fat and solemn. He took Vittoria's hand and held it for a long time in his own. Then he tested the stiffness of her arms and neck. Finally he put a hand between her teeth. 'Bite, Satan, if you have the courage,' he shouted into the face of the frightened child. The incense was lit in the thurible and the priest murmured incomprehensible litanies. Vittoria, amidst the smoke of the incense, thought she could glimpse her father's face.

'What do you want from me?' she asked him. But her tongue stumbled over the words and the onlookers perceived only inarticulate sounds. Her father remained mute, looking at his daughter with a mild expression.

'If you come back I swear I'll learn to play the violin,' said Vittoria; 'I know you like music so much. Why didn't you send me to a teacher?' Then he answered with gentle words; and Vittoria felt a faint caress on her cheeks. 'Don't worry about anything,' he said. 'You are my favourite, I love you even if you can't play the violin. Don't worry about anything.'

After the exorcism Vittoria spoke to her father several more times, but didn't manage to extract the promise of a return in the near future. After this their conversations became more rare and stopped at around her fifteenth year, when her schoolteachers convinced her that there is no return from death and that the dead don't talk.

Everything seemed to assert the contrary: the words of the poets, her own personal experience. But the teachers said no and in the end Vittoria believed them, or at least she appeared to believe. Because the moment she set eyes on the pages of the philosophers, in which heaven, hell, ghosts and the living merged into a single great design, an infinite fabric that rolled from the loom of unknowable weavers, Vittoria finally had an explanation for her childhood memories. And if her father's face no longer came back to visit her, and if her dreams were no longer peopled with unknown faces, she attributed this to a new insensitivity in her mind, sterilized – as she thought – by the scalpel of those officially charged with extirpating the magic from every adolescent heart.

I have now reached the final part of my story, and must overcome the greatest obstacle. It is like a rock, obstructing the path of thoughts and words. I have rolled it far away to tell you everything I know about myself, what I remember of my life. I am opening up the dark lair into which fate had chased me to make you understand that life really is full of hope, right down to the last breath.

Until the age of thirty-five I had lived as though in a confused dream. I saw chimeras fluttering about, faint and fleeting visions flashed before my eyes.

As a child I met soldiers running with their fists clenched, black-hearted priests who preached fasting and obedience. I saw damp basements pullulating with hiding men, houses demolished, hospital beds. Then, above my head there arose a new world: fierce men – former servants – uttered disdainful words. And others, those who were now the servants, waited slyly in ambush. The walls were raised again, the basements returned to their state of cold abandon.

Twenty years of schooling followed. Twenty years of empty words passed away. I learned of the movement of the stars, elliptical calculus and the volume of cubes, of Alexander the Great and God, I heard talk of insects and philosophers. Now I could repeat nothing of any of it, except vague and dull phrases. All that remains of all that is this shy alignment of phrases on a page, one after the other, in feverish confusion, for an unknown reader.

I became a clerk of court. On ruled and numbered sheets I noted down hostile conversations between judges and witnesses, desperate defences of imprisoned men. Once a week I went to prison to collect the complaints and confessions of the inmates. I remember the squeak of the iron door, the smell of mildew in the corridors of the former convent. Sometimes I would find myself in rooms involved with crimes, seeing corpses in unmade beds, bodies abandoned in the turmoil of the final moment by fleeing murderers. Or putting seals on the doors of abandoned dwellings, kaleidoscopes of lives that had ended badly.

I spent twenty more years like that. Judges, barely off the university benches when they assumed their office, turned white-haired before my eyes. Their respect for the law more and more often turned into a carapace, and their contempt for men became more and more lucid and cruel. Every now and again, in the law court, I would listen to the crowd shouting, as they waited for the

beginning of a trial, announcing the arrival of a prisoner. For me they were strangers, indistinct faces,
unapproachable creatures. The world outside? No, outside there was nothing. Everyone was guilty. Oh, all the
dry, vague testimonies to meaningless events.

A tiny typist, with tiny eyes, asked me for shelter one
evening. She told me her unhappy story of life with a
husband who was always drunk. I took her in. The next
day she brought her clothes to my place. We lived
together for ten years, until I found myself wanting to get
drunk as well.

Then humanity became sinister. The stammering of
the little thieves turned into shouts of hatred. The judges,
too, became ruthless. 'I request that the defendant be
given the maximum penalty,' they would have me write
in the registers. And the crowd shouted all the louder
during the hearings.

On the last day of that life I went to the bank. The
judge I was working with at that time wanted to ascertain
the origin of a cheque. I was carrying the document in a
black leather bag. That is all I can remember. A roaring
noise pierced my guts. I saw everything collapsing all
around, I saw expressions of terror. The explosion ripped
through my lungs.

I don't know how long I lay there unconscious, a
corpse among piles of corpses. In my dilated pupils was
fixed the vision of mutilated columns, shattered windows,
bodies in pieces. Then I closed my eyes.

I don't know how long the world ceased to exist for me. They tell me it was two months.

For that length of time I lay on a hospital bed with neither perceptions nor thoughts.

It was then that Vittoria came to my aid. What I am reporting here I learned from her and, to a lesser extent, from the doctors. I no longer trust the word of my friends. I don't know if I still have any.

Did Vittoria see Giacomo in me? Perhaps. Our bodies have shared similar fates, even if our souls have not. And what Vittoria could not do for him, she did for me. She stayed beside my bed, studying my breathing, stroking my face. I felt the caresses: not like those of a hand, but like a mysterious, beneficial fluid emanating from an ineffable and bodiless creature. Maybe God himself. No words could encompass that feeling; my being gradually became that sensation itself, an indistinct and beneficial flow, without time, without meaning, without any purpose but love.

What does that word mean: love? There is no point trying to explain it. Many people feel it, few acknowledge it. It's like stranger mingling, masked, among standing rows of people. No, I shall stop trying to tell you what I felt in those days and those nights. Only those who have crossed the great, dark river of fear, of death, of resurrection, will be able to understand.

Before Vittoria's healing caress I was ripped to pieces by hard and greedy hands. Other hands put my body together again, joining bone to bone, flesh to flesh. They beat me with hammers, divided me with saws and knives, searched among my fibres, weighed and filtered my blood, judged my soul. And still you ask what a caress is worth? What powers it has? And still you ask how you can cling to a smile when you emerge for a moment from the floods of non-being?

Yes, I clung to Vittoria's smile, when I opened my eyes. I saw her, pale. Her lips taut, imperceptibly turned upwards. Her narrow shoulders, her cheeks. Her slender torso. Her gentle eyes. Her children's clothes.

Vittoria brought me to her house when they sent me away from the hospital. I lay on her bed for more long weeks. She fed me. When my strength returned, we spoke. For a long time, for hours. She told me her life, just as I have done, but with more details, as though reliving it as she stood beside me, one moment after another. And I was the actor in her revocations. From one minute to the next I was her lover, her husband, her boyfriend. I felt that she was dressing me up – with her eyes – in each of their outfits, as little girls do with dolls, or puppeteers with marionettes. I felt myself changing now into an architect, now a painter. I even drew flowers and faces, I who until that moment could not even have traced the outlines of a 'naïve' painting.

Then I spoke. Not about my life: I didn't have one, I could barely remember my former life except with difficulty, as if through fog; but about imaginary worlds, perhaps unrepeatable, timeless and without events, without substance. They were worlds full of ghosts, which I had seen. Or worlds of fantasies, hallucinations and nightmares.

Thus, together, we created a new world, cementing her words with mine. These words are its genesis. And now we have been living there for a long, long time. We are the principal inhabitants. Often we meet other people there, other creatures. A cat, a lot of flowers. We listen to music, we applaud spectacles. It is as though we were part of a painting with motionless figures; as if this painting were constantly changing, but staying entirely motionless. Let us live. Let others think about time.

I am Vittoria's slave. In the evening I lie down at her feet in adoration. But I am also her master, when she covers me with flowers and kisses. I am her son and she is my daughter. I am my own ancestor, my own great-grandson. I am with her, the one who lives and sees. I have sometimes tried to look into the bottom of Vittoria's soul. But I have succeeded only once. Reading a sheaf of papers that she had left on a table. 'Playing the house game', that was what was written on the first page. I have jealously preserved that manuscript until today. But I would like everyone to see into Vittoria's soul: to catch sight of themselves, their own face. My face. *Amen.*

NOTE

There were thirty-nine of us in our class. Including wives, children and grandchildren, today I should be giving an account of two hundred and fifty individuals. I have put together brief notes about all of them. The publisher will be able to send a copy to anyone who asks for it.